FREE LOVE AND NICKEL BEER

FREE LOVE AND NICKEL BEER

THE LIFE AND TIMES OF DR. PAUL

———

Dr. Paul R. VeHorn, Ph.D.

DEDICATION

This book is dedicated to the three important women in my life:

Laura, Lillian, and Phebe

(My Grandmother, My Mother, and My Wife)

"All the world's a stage,
And all the men and women merely players;
They have their exits and entrances,
And one man in his time plays many parts."

William Shakespeare

CHAPTER 1

———◆———

THE WET NIGHT CRAWLER GLISTENED as it squirmed in the bottom of the black outside drain near my grandmother's rose garden. My almost three year old fingers reached for the wriggling worm. I quickly grabbed it and popped it into my mouth. Now I had seen robins do this dozens of times. So they must taste good, right?

"aaagh... yucky... aaagh... granma.. .aaagh!" I screamed.

As I bit down sour juices squirted on to my tongue while the sand grit from the worm's skin ground into my teeth.

My grandmothers freshly cut roses fell out of her apron as she ran to me.

" Paulie, Paulie, what are you eating?"

That was one of my earliest recollections. I never developed an interest in eating any type of worm thereafter, even one in the bottom of a bottle of Tequila. This is not meant to disparage Tequila however, since on a number of occasions, Tequila has added drama to my "life and times."

Near the end of WWII the Northern Indiana industrial town where I grew up was bustling. I lived with my mother and grandparents.

GI's were coming home from the war and times were great. The middle class was developing. Labor unions were thriving, UAW, IBEW, Steel Workers, AFL-CIO, and the Teamsters. Unlike now, the greed driven super rich were not looting the middle class.

"There's the cab!"

My grandmother was crying as my Uncle John got out of the cab in his Army uniform. He joined the Army at seventeen and a half, landed at Normandy on day two with Patton's third army division. He was in an armored anti tank unit known as "Hell on Wheels," very dangerous duty. These tanks were lightly armored with seventy five mm. guns and had a speed of forty mph. This was fast for a tank, but the idea was to go around and speed behind Nazi Panzer Tanks and shoot them from the rear where the Panzers were vulnerable, a dicey maneuver. Ultimately, he was awarded three bronze stars and the French Croix de Guerre. He turned down a battlefield commission. I guess he had his reasons. He only shared a few of those experiences with me after I was in the service. Combat Vets don't talk about their grisly war memories.

Uncle John's impact on my young life was formidable. Wow, was it ever! Now John truly looked like a movie star, he was studying music, and had a lyric tenor voice. The women loved him. This brings me to the next level of my boyhood experiences...and this step sure beat the hell out of biting a worm in two.

"Oh John, mmm, mmm,"

There they were...in my Grandmas kitchen dressed in their tennis outfits, kissing and embracing... (My Grandfather would call this necking)... and there I was at just six years old, watching while hiding behind the upstairs door. This would be my first experience as a voyeur. I was turned on, really turned on. In my young mind the feeling was better than anything ... almost as good as Christmas or maybe even better.

"Paulie, What are you doing?"

Oops....I was so focused I didn't hear my grandmother coming down the stairs. My first blushing brush with Eros suddenly slammed shut... only I wasn't blushing.. .I was shaking. Why is it we remember all the sexual experiences we have ever had... but I still can't quote the chapter and paragraph of a Bible verse.

"Oh grandma... I...uh... was just going to get some cookies and milk," I jumped.

By this time Uncle John and his erstwhile girl friend were casually talking. Later he actually thanked me and gave me money for the movies because he thought I warned him that Grandma was coming. I lucked out and he didn't have a clue... or did he... he kind of winked and smiled. Life went on with another memorable childhood experience soon to follow.

John Wayne wears a bra... what...John Wayne wears a bra? Well, the answer to that is yes, and no. You see it all happened when I saw the movie "Flying Tigers" with John Wayne. I knew right then that I was destined to become a fighter pilot. I could clearly see myself climbing into the cockpit of my Curtis Wright P-40 War hawk... the sinister teeth of a tiger shark painted on both sides of the front with mean searing eyes seeking out the enemy. The glorious adventure for an eight year old was about to begin. I donned my flying cap, goggles and headphones... ah yes...the headphones. I strode into my grandmother's summer kitchen where the chief mechanic was warming up my P-40. I could hear the roar of the engine as I felt the excitement of boarding, to head into the wild blue yonder.

My Flying Tiger cock pit was the wooden chair from a long ago dining room set laying on its back side with the legs spreading out behind. The seat was the back of my flight chair. I put one of my grandfather's life preserver boat cushions under my butt... good idea I thought... one never knows if he has to ditch into the sea. I hurriedly put on my winter cap which at that time looked exactly like a flight cap, and my swim goggles. This was real the real thing... and then I put on my headphones. I pulled back on the cut off broom stick... (Which was in reality my flight stick)... and just as I was lifting off the runway my grandmother opened the summer kitchen door... talk about flightus interruptus. I could hear the engine scream... that would be me making fighter plane sounds...whnn n n n -zoooooo<u>m</u>...airborne at last!...then...

"Paulie are you having fun?" My grandma sweetly asked.

"Oh my...oh my...oh my...oh my." Was suddenly all she could say.

I thought maybe she forgot something as she slammed the door on the way out of the summer kitchen. I just went on flying...I could hear the other pilots in my group firing at the enemy and cheering... as they shot down the Zeros. My head phones were perfect.

One of my mom's bras fit perfectly over both of my ears... and there was a snap under my chin. John Wayne should be so lucky. I finally landed, exhausted from having shot down at least a dozen enemy planes. I removed my flight gear and walked through the porch into the kitchen of the house. My mom had just come home from work.

"Paul, go to your room," My mother ordered.

I noticed my grandmother was upset...she had been crying. I wondered what happened. Maybe somebody in the family had died. I heard my grandmother talking to mom.

"Oh I hope he is not going to be one of those...they have such a hard life you know...Beatrice's grandson is one...it's so sad...Paulie's father is not in his life...that can happen," grandma went on.

I did not have the foggiest idea what they were talking about. Pretty soon mom came upstairs to my room. She looked both concerned, and angry as she sat down on the bed. I was sitting on the floor playing with a P-40 model airplane. I really remember it as if it happened just an hour ago.

"What were you doing in the summer kitchen?" She sternly asked.

"I was flying my P-40 Flying Tiger."

Mom paused, with a look that said grandma had gotten got something wrong.

"Just what were you doing with my bra over your head young man?" Mom' s face was getting red.

"You mean that thing you put on over...you know...your things?" I thought...uh oh.

"You know what a bra is," mom was getting angry.

I knew I better have a quick answer, "those are my headphones."

Mom looked like a deer caught in the headlights.

"Yeah...so I can hear the other pilots when they shoot down a plane."

In retrospect mom's reaction was kind of funny. She couldn't quite get the connection at first...then she finally got it.

"I will buy you a pair of ear muffs that look like head phones, but no more of that playing with my bras, do you understand?"

"Yes ma' am."

Mom went back downstairs to the kitchen. By that time my grandfather was home. I heard a lot of quiet talking that I couldn't make out. Then suddenly I heard my grandfather roar with laughter. He could hardly stop. I heard later that my whole family heard the story...a story which probably still remains in that Northern Indiana city's historical museum... the day that John Wayne wore a bra.

Kids were more enterprising then. The age of sitting on your ass playing games in front of a computer screen had not as yet arrived... thank God. A few kids were obese, but very few.

"Hey Paulie, I'm open," Jimmy yelled.

I dribbled the basketball a few more times before handing it off to let him score. The early March winds made the freezing temperatures cut even more. The alley was filled with a half dozen kids shooting hoops in a pickup game of basketball. Sometimes slipping on the ice, the after school crowd would squeeze in about forty five minutes of light to play the sport. In Indiana, basketball is known as Hoosier hysteria... game over, Jimmy and I walked home.

"Hey, my brother is getting a paper route, and I'm gonna help him." Jimmy was excited.

"Oh yeah...how much is he paying you?"

He said there were ninety papers to deliver on the rout each evening after school and they would each take half. That gave me an idea.

"Let me go with you on your route, I want to see how it's done."

"You mean for free?"

"Yeah, just to see how it works."

I went with them for a couple weeks. Some evenings it snowed...a couple evenings it rained... the job really was a job.

"Grandma I want to go into business."

Now my grandmother could pinch a buffalo nickel till it mooed. She always kept a sharp eye out for a business opportunity. In fact, when I was selling Christmas cards for the school she set up all of her friends, and our relatives to buy cards...or else. Needless to say I won.

"What kind of business?" She asked me seriously.

"I want a newspaper route."

"Mrnmm, I'll talk to your grandfather."

And talk to him she did...the very next day after school my grandfather took time off work and met me. We walked about half a mile to the tallest bank building in the city. On the bottom floor were the offices of Merrill, Lynch, Pierce, Fenner and Smith (now known simply as Merrill Lynch). As soon as we walked into the large office I was totally fascinated.

"What are all those numbers flashing along the top of the wall?" I asked.

Over the din and the noise he explained what the symbols meant and what business stocks were all about. He even introduced me to his stock broker.

"I was a paper boy at one time, that's a good way to begin." He went on to explain how business worked.

Little did I know then that one day I would become a series seven stock broker, insurance broker and real estate agent. It was so exciting to me that I had chills running down my back. What a wonderful thing it was for my grandfather to take his time to do that...I later found out that my grandmother ' suggested' it.

"I have been delivering this paper route now for about five months, and I want two more routes." I said.

The district manager looked at me as if I had lost my marbles.

"I am doing a good job, right?"

"Sure, but how are you going to handle three routes?" He asked.

"None of the paper boys like to collect the money, so I will pay them to deliver the papers and I'll collect the money."

He said he would get back with me on that. There was no joy to shlep through the route each day rain, snow or shine, so I came up with that idea. Not only did he get back with me, he gave me a total of six routes to manage.

"So now you have six guys working for you, how does it feel?"

"It feels great and I know I can do it."

It turned out to be a three year education about people and business that could never be learned in a classroom.

———•———

CHAPTER 2

"PUT YOUR BOOTS ON PAULIE and don't forget your lunch tickets."

"OK grandma... hey grandpa didn't shovel the snow off the sidewalk."

"One day soon that will be your job."

Now Northern Indiana was no place to be in the winter, and I had just helped grandpa shovel the snow last week at eighteen degrees Fahrenheit. That was no fun. I trudged along to school as the sparkling snow crunched beneath my four buckle arctic boots.

"Billy... Billy," I called. A boy came tumbling down the stairs of his house, his mother standing behind the door. He and I walked to school together.

"Hey Paulie, the preacher is going to teach our religion class today"… he warned... "so don' t be a smart ass,"... he laughed.

This was the oldest and most prestigious Lutheran Church in the city. My mother and Aunts and Uncles also went to this school. It was founded as a German Lutheran Church and school in the eighteen hundreds. Of course the family attended every Sunday. To my knowledge they don't ordain women to this day. My fond and not so fond memories of my childhood happened there for nine years from Kindergarten through eighth grade.

I would go to church with Mom on Sundays before I was old enough to go to Sunday school. I was between four and five years old at the time. My penchant for being an entertainer began at that tender age. Although I am now in SAG/AFTRA my debut into the wonderful world of show biz was less than pleasant. This was in the day when preachers didn't know when to stop. A church service would last for over two hours.

Now being a perceptive child I readily recognized that a fog of boredom wafted across the congregation. Bring on the entertainment...and it was show time for me. Mom was sitting next to me so I had to be cool. She would be looking at the preacher, her eyes glazed over as if she were thinking about her date from last night and I went to work. Turning sideway in my seat, it was just enough to cross my eyes and stick out my tongue. Not everyone can do that at the same time I understand... at least I thought so at the time. Hell, there are people today who can't walk and chew gum at the same time. If the men hadn't chuckled so loud, Mom would never have known...or maybe it was when their wives gave me dirty looks and their husbands groaned when their wives elbowed them in the ribs that gave me away. I was very tenacious. Mom would stop me but I felt it was my God given duty to save these souls from the Hell of boredom in church....so I would do it again.

The "licken" house was a small red brick building which actually was the ladies room. But it looked like a building you would see in a Nazi POW camp. I swear I once saw a WWII movie with that very building in a POW camp. I call it the "licken" house because that's what Mom had appropriately named it. You see, when I would practice my theatrics in church, Mom would take me to the dreaded "licken" house after church... where I would get a "licken"... and not an easy one either. My grandma was not there to save me...now grandma was the queen of the entire family.. .and I was the fair haired boy...the only child...the prince... and woe unto he... or she... who would trifle with me. After every one of these ordeals I would walk home from church with mom and hang back. When we would get home I would "tell" grandma... not just tell... but using all of the stage skills I could muster I would "present" what happened. My grandfather actually enjoyed the show...my grandmother on the other hand took my part and promised me two desserts for Sunday dinner... that did not please mom.

"Lillian, you spank him so much at church that when he grows up he won't go to church," grandma said to mom.

Grandma was so right, but it had not so much to do with the afore said "licken" house as it did with dogma... in fact, my karma ran over my dogma... Oh yes, in case you were wondering, spanking your kids was perfectly legal at that time and even recommended.

In fact if I was spanked at school, my grandfather would be called and I would get spanked again at home for getting in trouble at school... grandpa's razor strap had a lot of miles on it from my mom and all the aunts and uncles...as well as me... I can honestly say that I probably deserved more spankings than I got.

A razor strap is a three inch wide by twenty four inch long leather strap which is used to hone a straight razor. I don't know how they did it, but men actually shaved clean mostly without a knick.

Now this strap hung threateningly behind the bathroom door. That strap seemed to threaten everyone with the exception of my Uncle Fred who became a hero in the book of family lore. It seems that one snowy evening he trudged home from school. At eight years old he was in third grade at the aforementioned German Lutheran grade School... AKA... 'the crazy house' ... now well documented... where he had received a spanking.

The U.S. Army had apparently missed this spanker who obviously had been a member in good standing of the Gestapo... or was he here before the war... anyway it must have been in his DNA. This guy actually had a German accent which sounded like that of a Nazi U Boat Commander. On top of that he had to be eight feet tall... or seemed that way when even I had him at the same school. He was notorious for inflicting corporal punishment for even any minor infraction. So Uncle Fred got the business... of course in front of the class. Mr. Gestapo liked Uncle Fred so much that he remembered him. Unfortunately when I was in this torture meister's class he found out that I was the nephew...I never did, but I need to thank Unc for that one.

When my grandfather came home from work and heard that Uncle Fred was spanked at school he went to fetch the feared and deeply hated razor strap. Only the strap wasn't in its usual place. As I understand it grandma was cooking dinner and had a roast in the oven. The story goes that she thought something was burning... so she opened the oven door... and something was burning.. .it was the hated razor strap... only this time *it* was hated and heated... to a crisp. It all but crumbled when she removed it from the oven... in pieces.

One would think that Uncle Fred would have become a chef after that stunt. Alas no, but he *did* get his spanking postponed as did all of his brothers and sisters until grandpa bought a new razor strap... which by the way came out of Fred's allowance.

Thus another chapter in the book of family lore comes to a courageous end... thanks to Uncle Fred.

CHAPTER 3

———◆———

AFTER A COLD ONE MILE plus trek, Billy and I finally arrived at school. When we entered our classroom the students were already standing at attention waiting for the minister to arrive.

"Good morning boys and girls."

"Good morning reverend Johan" (not his real name of course)

"You may take your seats."

Confirmation classes were being held by the pastor in order to impress us with the sacrament of communion as a rite of passage into the church.

"This morning our lesson will be about the beginning, Adam and Eve... they were the only persons on earth and they begat children"

We all knew what that meant and a couple boys had to stand in the comer for snickering…the reverend droned on.

"The Bible says in Genesis that they were fruitful and multiplied and replenished the earth."

I raised my hand at "fruitful and multiplied"... everyone looked... they didn't know what to expect... I had no idea at that time that I would one day be in MENSA... thus I was for all intents and purposes known as a smart ass... my classmates loved it... but the faculty and the preacher...not so much... nothing really bad but always on the edge... for nine years old I had already read things I should not have read... and I am not just talking about " Tijuana Bibles"... (for the twenty-first century reader those are sex comic books)... although I had found my uncles stash... another story... but I read my mother' s medical research bulletins as well. The question I asked the preacher that day... and his subsequent answer... changed my religious beliefs forever.

"Reverend Johan if Adam and Eve were the first people on earth and they had children who were fruitful and multiplied ... (now wait for it)... does that mean that they married their brothers and sisters?"

Suddenly the earth stood still...a hush fell over the classroom... I could see on the face of my classmates that they were expecting the wrath of God to nail me on the spot... doom and gloom filled the air.

"Well, Paul, see me after class."

My thoughts were of my grandfather having to come to school to not only meet with a teacher or even the principal, but with the Reverend himself...I would have Hell to pay.

"Alright class that's the bell now leave the room, Paul you stay, come to the desk" "Yes, reverend Johan"

At that moment I thought he was going to take his belt off and bend me over the desk.. .I wouldn't be able to sit down for a week... then they would tell my grandfather. .. that would be another week...but no.. .I couldn't believe it...the preacher started talking to me... he was condescending ... as he sat behind the desk with his elbows on top and his fingers of either hand touching each other.

"Well now Paul, there are certain things we take on faith and we won't think or talk about that again will we."

"No Reverend Johan, never again," I said.

That's when I knew.. .I discovered it...religions make things up as they go along...I started reading even more...I read about the early church... the Knights Templar.. .the Reformation... the Spanish inquisition... the burning of witches in New England...by the time I reached ten years old and beyond for the rest of my life I decided to believe in God but to not believe in religion. When callers on my show ask me what my religion is I simply say I'm a theosophist. .. meaning I believe there is an element of truth in most religions... works for me.

I was smitten. For some reason that morning as I walked through the Fall leaves on my way to school I had a really heady feeling. Even at nine years old I had a kind of sixth sense. Ah yes, the first day of seventh grade, and I was looking forward to it.

To this day the picture of her is a digital memory in my mind. As I walked into the classroom I saw her from her left side. A beige dress smoothly covered her slender curves while her long dark hair slid over her shoulders. The face... ah the face of pure symmetry with a light carotene complexion that reminded me of Hawaiian hula girls I had seen in a movie. As she turned her head toward me her deep intense brown eyes and perfect smile said something... to me.

"And what is your name?"

" uh... uh... I... er."

I knew I had a name... I had a name when I walked in... I had a library card with my name on it... but it had probably melted in my wallet along with the rest of me.

"Paul... uh Paul... uh Paul VeHorn."

"Alright Paul you sit right over here."

The location couldn't have been better... first row to her right. I guess she thought she could keep an eye on me. Better yet, I could keep an eye on her... heh... heh.

Miss Doulet... not her real name for purposes of this book, but you get the idea. I saw that her teeth were perfect, so I decided to tell Mom that I wanted the braces on right away. I had to look my best for Miss Doulet. I further decided that I would really be "Ajay Squared Away" (a cartoon character at that time) and stay on her good side. No smart ass with her. This was it. I was a new guy... inspired by what was to become my image of what a beautiful... no... better than that... a gorgeous woman was.

I was an only child and precocious. Adults and older kids were always around and learning about sex by listening was a skill I perfected. Movies were becoming more risqué after WWII and I was at the neighborhood theatre every Saturday. Forbidden fruit is the sweetest and the "verboten" of" verbotens" was sex and any of its fellow travelers. Of course hypocrisy ran rampant in America at that time... just like now... the more things change the more they remain the same.

Although I wasn't aware of it at the time I now know that the politics of sex, beautiful women and jealousy can be very ugly. The cable series "Mad Men" illustrates that perfectly. An attractive teacher in a church school setting is a train wreck ready to happen.

When the first back to school parent/teacher night took place more men attended the event than ever before. The students attended too but we went to the gym. I didn't realize until later that the male interest in this seventh grade beauty was her undoing. She was a perfect lady but the witches that burned her were the "good ladies" of the church. Miss Doulet was gone before the end of the first semester.

My grandmother, born in Germany, was a liberal and fair person. Grandma was Protestant, but her father was born Jewish and converted. As a result my grandmother was familiar with Yiddish and would frequently use Yiddish words because she said they were just more exact... However, Yiddish is considered to be "The Mother's Language."

She commented that she would have nothing to do with those "alter yenta" which I understand means old gossips.

So Miss Doulet began teaching in the public school system. Churches have a way of paying as little as possible to their employees all the while being tax exempt. Fortunately her income was increased and when I heard that I felt happy for her. Better than that, the "alter yenta" were seething because Miss Doulet went to church every Sunday. My grandmother loved it. .. so did my grandfather but for obviously different reasons. The best part was that I always tried to see her after church and say hello... and my heart skipped a beat every time she said... "Hello Paulie" ... she called me Paulie... I loved it.

CHAPTER 4

———◆———

MY UNCLE WILLY (WILLIAM) WAS an adventure to know. He always had a wad of tobacco in his mouth and a cuss word on his lips. At the same time he was sentimental to a fault and often had a tear in his eye. A rough sort to be sure. At one time he owned a candy factory but sold the recipes and decided to work for someone else.

Every Sunday morning, rain, shine, or snow he would walk a mile to my grandparent's home and he and my grandfather would walk another mile to church. In the meantime grandmother would ride to church with my uncle. Now this is an important point because Uncle Willy had never perfected the fine art of spitting tobacco... my grandmother wouldn't even think of accompanying someone with base manners such as his even though he was her brother and she loved him. She came from a very successful and well bred family, but Uncle Willy was the so called black sheep of the family. He was a great guy and had great stories for a kid of nine years old to hear.

My grandfather and Uncle Willy would walk together side by side almost at a march step.. .I would have to nearly run along behind or try to squeeze in next to them on the sidewalk. The latter was a bad idea since Uncle Willy would always spit to his right... now remember that for future reference... we' re having a pop quiz at the end of this book.

"That was a Hell of a sermon Reverend Johan"

"Why thank you Willy, I am glad you enjoyed it."

I kid you not... word for word and that's what he would tell the preacher when he really liked the sermon... and this gloriously hot Sunday morning was no exception.

"Hey Dad, Uncle Willy, it' s a hot day let me drive you home."

My uncle by marriage, Uncle George was about six foot four and played football in school. He always drove a big car, usually the biggest Buick he could buy. They already had three kids but my aunt was expecting again. On this Sunday, my two older cousins were with him at church so we all piled into the car. Now you need to appreciate the seating arrangement. Uncle George was driving, my grandfather sat in the front seat middle, and my Uncle Willy sat at the window seat.

"Aw VeHorn, you got to sit in the middle it' s my dad' s car."

My cousin Ritchie was a whiney sort. You would think that by ten years old he would have grown out of that... but he used the whiney to get his way... and he was the youngest in his family…so far. He loved to lord it over me because he was a year older. He wasn' t the brightest light on the Christmas tree, and I always made top grades. He hated that because my aunt and my mother would com-pare grades and he would catch it. It was even better that we both were in the same school.

That put my older cousin by three years Mikey next to the window in the back seat behind my Uncle George…I was in the middle of the back seat and my cousin Ritchie a year older than me at the window behind Uncle Willy. It was a fine summer day… a day when all the windows of a car were rolled down because cars in Northern Indiana did not need air conditioning or so they thought.

As we were driving I saw the back of Uncle Willy's head arch to the right and I heard the smack of spitting lips as the long brown string of tobacco juice snapped into the open back window and splat onto my cousin's face.

"Whaaa… whaaa… aaaagh."

The shrieking coming from the mouth of Ritchie's now tobacco stained face was nothing less than the souls of the dead in the torture of Hell. But wait…at that same time I heard the sound of orgasmic laughter coming from my left. My cousin Mikey was laughing his ass off…bad idea Mikey…I caught a glimpse of my grandfather as he looked back at me as if to say don't even think about laughing… then an enormous wind passed by my face… Uncle George was livid…the wind I felt was the palm of his hand rushing past my face to connect with my other cousins face… the contact was so loud it echoed… WHAP… and what was Uncle Willy's comment? I'm sorry…no… Are you OK…absolutely not… and not even a…do you want a hankie?

"Dumb kid," grumped Uncle Willy.

As we got out of the car at my grandparent's home I could see Uncle George was so mad his face was crimson. The two boys were crying like in a duet…big boo hoos… and sobbing.

As soon as they drove off my grandfather couldn't hold it. He laughed so hard he almost swallowed his false teeth. I was laughing too as we walked into the kitchen. Uncle Willy usually stayed over after church for a shot of schnapps with my grandfather, but I guess this time he just thought it was prudent to not face my grandmother.

"You didn't laugh about that did you Paulie?"

"No grandma, not until we came home."

The kid's paradise of summer vacation was on us once again. June brought the deliverance of my new cousin... but I had another problem. Uncle George brought my two cousins to grandmas because my aunt was at the hospital having the baby.

Grandma would bake cookies on Wednesday... she would bake so many cookies that they would last through the following week. Grandma was more than a cook...she was a master chef. Her cookies were topped with bright multi colored sugar that would melt in your mouth like fudge sickles on a hot summer day. But today was not just any Wednesday... it was black Wednesday because my cousins would be at grandmas that meant fewer cookies for me... and those schweine would slop at the cookie trough until none were left... all gone... every last sweet crisp crumb.

"Granny's gonna make sugar cookies today," said Mikey grinning.

Gothcha...I thought. Mikey was about two sandwiches short of a full picnic. His laughter sounded crazed... as in perfect for Halloween. I knew grandma hated the word Granny... and Mikey knew it too. In fact the word granny was way beneath my grandmother's dignity.

A diabolical plan formulated in my devious mind. I went into the house.. .grandma was in the kitchen.

"Grandma, what does granny mean," I asked.

"Paul (she only said Paul when she was being stem, otherwise it was Paulie) where did you hear that?"

"Well Mikey said granny was going to bake sugar cookies today."

"I am just going to have to wait until tomorrow to bake cookies, I have too much to do today."

Grandma set her schedule like a field marshal. She was a Capricorn, and nothing would change her mind set... except it would seem for the word "granny." She was exact in her timing. On bitterly cold Wednesdays after school, the scent of fresh baked cookies would waft through the house as I ate oven warm cookies and drank cool milk. It didn't get any better than that.

But this was June and the cookie gods had just smiled on me.. .it was going to be a great summer.

At last, eighth grade. The final year at the place we not so affectionately called the "unksemeinde" which we said meant crazy house in German but it really didn't.

However, it wasn't a good idea to get caught saying, writing or even thinking that word on campus.

The school principal taught grade eight. He already had a rather dim view of me and was convinced that I was flirting with his fiancé who was also on the faculty. She would sometimes substitute in our class. He once called in my mother about my flirting with the girls...actually that was a two way street. Although I didn't' see it then, here was an adult male who was so insecure that he thought a twelve year old boy was flirting with his fiancé. He was right of course, but even then I mostly did it to annoy him since she was no great beauty... I really think she was flattered.

CHAPTER 5

———•———

IT WAS THE FIRST DAY of High School at the most prestigious Protestant Academy in Northern Indiana... ah, the thought of football games and bonfires... dances and girls... cold autumn nights driving in open convertibles... but not today. The day from Hell was quickly upon me.

My knees got wet when I was forced to kneel in front of the commode. As the apples floated in the boy's locker room toilet I tried to grab them with my teeth. Freshman hazing was alive and well in this Protestant High School. While my ROTC uniform tie dragged in the water upper classmen were screaming.

"Get your god dam head down in that toilet Horny or I'll push your face in it."

There... he said it...the name that would stick with me forever, along with VeHorny, Veryhorny, and of course Perv since my initials are PRV. I learned to exploit those names especially when I was called them in the company of women. I discovered that it definitely pays to advertise.

The tormentors went to another stall; I yanked my right hand out of the back of my waist band. They had tightened my belt hard sticking my hands in the back. I was ready to gag, but managed to grab an apple, stick it in my mouth, and stay on my knees while quickly jamming my right hand back into the pants waist again.

My harassers returned as quickly as they had left. "get up... stand up plebe... now you run through the halls to your next class just like that... you try to take that apple out of your mouth we're going to kick your ass."

The objective was to not let the upperclassmen drag you into the latrine between classes. Lesson learned, and the first day of high school was one for the books. Oh yeah...lest I forget... later that day one of the student officers gigged me for having a wet tie. He was one of the same inquisitors from the toilet scene.

It must have been in an effort to keep expenses down that caused this prestigious Protestant high school to hire a joke as the required military officer to be in charge of the ROTC program. This clod came right out of a Dickens novel. The word was that he was never on active duty even during the war... 4F I would think... but somehow he got appointed to the Army National Guard of the state as a captain. Keep in mind that the Guard at that time was often filled with political appointees.

Graham Wilson has always been one of my favorite cartoonists. I remember one Playboy Holiday issue with Santa Claus at the door of a little boy's bedroom. The boy looks scared stiff. There is an overweight Santa with a big meaty mean face an ugly smile and crooked teeth saying, "I hear you've been a bad little boy Johnny." That was him. Wilson nailed it. If ever there was a caricature of someone, this was it. This was our captain.

As if he weren't pathetic enough, this oaf had established a title for himself that came right out of a West Point textbook. Are you ready...I kid you not... PMS&T... Professor of Military Science and Tactics.. .I doubt if this jerk had ever attended college let alone be qualified as a "PMS&T." This pathetic poseur couldn't find his big fat ass with both hands. Captain DA (for dumbass as we called him) was in his glory. It gets better. He carried a swagger stick, and just lorded or larded over the cadets. Now every bully needs a toady... just like in the film "A Christmas Story"... and Captain Dumbass had his.

You probably guessed it, another Army National Guard Soldier. I say soldier out of respect because he had been on active duty during WWII. When he returned home he joined the Guard. D.A. was smart enough to know that he needed a real military member to train the cadets. We called him Corporal Red because he had a shock of red hair shaped into a perfect "flat top" style. He was all discipline but we liked him. He taught us how to fire expert on the rifle range. Three days a week you had to fire expert before you could leave the range. That paid off for me later.

Unfortunately Red had to brown nose D.A., and whenever credit was to be taken for the cadet corps D.A. took it. He was nauseating... even a freshman cadet could see what was going on. We would win rifle matches with Red having trained us and D.A. would get the glory. Life goes on.

Athlete's foot was an affliction that was hard to get rid of at that time, and all the cadets sharing the shower room didn't help matters. I had the misfortune of getting a really serious case. Our family doctor wrote prescriptions and a note which stated that I had to wear white socks. The Army ROTC uniform called for black socks.

Tears of anger were streaming down my cheeks... it seemed like the entire student body was in the hall way watching. This was a co-ed school but ROTC was mandatory for the boys. I could see that some of the girls were crying as Captain Dumb Ass was giving me a dressing down.

"I don't give a damn what your doctor says... I don' t give a damn about his note... you're nothing but a sniveling little cry baby...now get out of my sight...report to the principal."

He said more... a lot more...but you get the idea. If he had pulled that crap today some kid would have come back to school with a gun. Needless to say I hated his guts, but all bullies get theirs in the end. Remember Uncle John?

The scent of burning leaves filled the air, and the smell of pumpkin pies wafted through the house on that Sunday before Thanksgiving. Uncle John went to school on the G.I. Bill in Chicago and came home for the Holiday.

I never quite saw him look like this before. His blues eyes turned to steel grey. Some people get angry and become fiery... not Uncle John... it wasn't his fire that you had to fear...it was his ice.

"I'll go to school with you tomorrow... early... very early." He never said another word about it.

Now, my parents were divorced and my dad lived in California. My uncles and my grandfather tried to be father figures as best as they could. I was more like a little brother to Uncle John. I later found out that he had carried my picture in his wallet through-out Europe while fighting the Nazis. I really appreciated learning about that...a couple years ago I went to visit him in Chicago before he passed away. It was then that he pulled out his wallet and showed me the picture of a little guy with a big smile... he carried it all of his life. I held back the tears until later.

Very few people were around, but we marched ... and I do mean marched or at least it seemed that way, to the principal's office. The principal came in as we sat in the outer office. Uncle John introduced himself in a very crisp military manner...business like at best... and cold at worst... Virtually everyone in the area knew about John' s war time heroism. The local paper had featured a number of local WWII Veterans and their decorations.

"Mr. (principal) I want an immediate meeting with you and Capt. (name)"

"Well, I'll have to ask him what his schedule... "

"You have a choice, you either get him here now or we can take it up with my attorney in Chicago."

Now the word attorney causes some people to get a knot in their knickers. Combine that with "from Chicago" and the term "immediate" has a whole new impact.

"Mrs. (secretary) have Capt. (you know) come to my office immediately".

Corporal Red, the toady, opened the door for D.A. They saw me in the waiting room when D.A. sneered, "in trouble again VeHorn?"

My Uncle was already sitting unseen through the frosted windows of the Principals office. The secretary directed Red and me to stay in the outer office.

"I expect my aide to accompany me." D.A. said not knowing about the Hell he was going to catch. (You recall that my Uncle's anti-tank unit was called "Hell on Wheels")

"Not this time Captain," The principal sounded nervous.

Red sat across from me. We could hear it begin. D.A. started to yell as if he were in charge. We could see that my Uncle stood up. Then D.A. stood up… John told him to sit down and shut up before he knocked him down. We could see that D.A. sat down, quickly. I then looked at Red… and I swear a smirk crossed his lips. There was more of course but we couldn't hear most of it.

From that day forward Capt. Dumbass did his very best to avoid me. He never looked at me. I never mentioned the incident to my fellow cadets. However, they all knew, the staff knew and best of all Red was there. From then on whenever I would encounter Red in the hall he would just look at me as a slight smile played across his mouth. Red and I had established a camaraderie.

CHAPTER 6

———◆———

THE DRAGONS RUNNING THROUGH THE palmettos scared the hell out of me as I walked to my new High School. They were in fact not dragons at all, but little and not so little lizards common to the State of Florida.

Sadly, my beloved grandmother had passed away. Since my grand-parents had spent the winters on the West Coast of Florida, my grandfather decided to move there. Along with my mother, and grandfather I was now living in a new world.

It was hot that August morning as I walked through the empty hall of this beautiful new high school. Classes would start in ten days and I had to enroll now. I saw a man who I later found out was one of the lawn maintenance men.

"Hi, can you tell me where the drinking fountain is?"

" Yezer, it be right up der on yer right."

"Thanks." I said with some surprise.

Mmm... Thought... he called me sir...shortly I remembered... I was now in the South. There were two water fountains... with two signs... one sign said "white only" and the other said "colored". I thought it was probably wise to drink from the "white only" fountain... although just to be a smart ass I thought about drinking from the "colored" fountain.

I had heard about segregation but I had never really witnessed it until now. We all went to school together, played ball together and got along as kids usually do in Northern Indiana. Not one kid in this school was African American... this is a current term... the "N" word was more or less common then and colored was the "acceptable" term. Most of the students and teachers were "transplanted Yankees" as we were called. I guess it really didn't register with me that there were actually teachers and students in this school who were really staunch segregationists. I later made one big mistake by not realizing what the repercussions could be by not conforming to the system.

Everything was going along like magic... it was like I hit the lottery of life. I had my own car, a Ford I called "Maybelline," we spent nearly every week end at the beach together. This was California South it seemed at the time. The Gulf of Mexico on the West Coast of Florida was a treasure... beautiful sunsets.. .walking hand in hand down the beach... a full moon that made the water shimmer... the bikinis... The rock & roll music... what a life.

At that point in time a first car was the singular most important step to adulthood and freedom. My listeners and viewers have called in periodically to say my tribute to Maybelline brought back wistful memories of their first cars. Are you ready to be wistful?

When I first saw her she smiled at me...her name was Maybelline... her color was money green. I wouldn't tell a lady's age but her vintage was 1953 making her one of the last flat head V-8s that Ford had made.. .she already belonged to someone else but I knew that I was her first true love... and she was mine... she met me after her 6th. Year... at my sixteen and a half years we were a perfect match.. .her glass pack mufflers purred... but she would roar just right when I down shifted while cruising around the local drive- in... she knew when the other girls were watching... she went everywhere with me... to school... to football games... to the super market where I worked part time (I would buy her nice things like white sidewall tires, seat covers and radio speakers)...to my favorite Gulf beach (she loved to go there with me, windows down, and her radio playing Beach Boys songs).. .taking girls on dates (but she didn't mind she knew we were one)... the prom... high school graduation... she was always there for me... then the day came for me to leave for the service...her gleaming moon hubcaps and shiny tail pipes... she seemed to glow that day... as I walked around in front of her I'm sure she smiled at me... a knowing smile...a sad smile.. .I never really saw her again... but I do see her...under that palm tree where we would park at the beach... when I drive by the high school...I've seen her waiting for me in the parking lot...Maybelline will always be a part of me.

CHAPTER 7

AT THAT TIME THE MILITARY draft faced every male at eighteen years of age. In fact you had to sign up with the selective service administration or face fines and/or imprisonment. Most college bound students would opt to join a military reserve program which required at least six months active duty and five and a half years of active reserve. That meant one meeting per week or one week-end per month and two weeks of active duty a year.

Otherwise one could get a student deferment as long as the grade point average was at least a C. The Army Reserve and Army National Guard offered the six month active duty program. The Navy Reserve offered a minimum of two years at that time plus four years of active reserve. For the majority it was six months active duty... out... and on to school.

I share this with the reader to not bore you but to set you up for what is coming. In retrospect echoes of Heller's book, "Catch 22" resonated throughout my experiences in the Florida Army National Guard (FLANG). By the way, if you have not read "Catch 22" do so ASAP.

I have heard that there are lies, damn lies and statistics. Nay nay... statisticians cannot hold a candle to military recruiters...ever!

My goal was to acquire a double major in communications and psychology. A communications degree in journalism and broadcasting with a psychology major to boot was a ticket to the broadcast industry. I had a great high school guidance counselor who recommended that plan for me. I was on it with just a minor six month delay in the service. Always be careful of the word "minor."

At that time Fort Monmouth New Jersey was THE class "A" school for all service branches to send personnel who were going to be public information specialists. The PIO (public information office) in every branch was a high echelon position even for enlisted members.

"Mr. VeHom," the recruiter at the Florida Army National Guard addressed me as mister... he knew exactly how to make a seventeen and a half year old feel important.

"Your armed forces qualifying test and high school records show you can enter that PIO training at Fort Monmouth. We can make that happen. That Army Reserve unit can't do that... they have only medical and transportation divisions. At Fort Monmouth you' ll receive concentrated training...it' ll be like finishing your first year of college."

What a great huge stinking pile of "Toro Fecundi" that turned out to be. I swear that I heard satanic laughter in the back of my mind as he spoke. Talk about being devious, this guy was an expert. Wait for it...because the best part of this Florida Army National Guard saga is yet to come. Of course this recruiter got his ill gotten bonus for enlisting another gullible, bright eyed, trusting, and naïve teenager.

In retrospect, my first experiences in the FLANG were at best a bad joke. I was issued ill fitting used, but at least clean uniforms.

I was also issued used field equipment including a mess kit which had the name Pyle as in Ernie Pyle deeply scratched on the back... could this have belonged to the great war journalist?...who knows... but at least I felt at the time that it was a good omen. I was told I wouldn't receive new uniforms until I went on active duty. In the meantime my friends who joined the U.S. Army reserve received all new uniforms and equipment.

High school continued to be cool and I spent one evening per week at National Guard reserve meetings. These meetings were dull and boring consisting of cleaning weapons and equipment. About once a month we would watch "skin flicks" or "fuck movies," as some of the guys would say, and they would pass around a bottle of vodka. If you had a military ID card drinking was perfectly legal. Now these movies were not of the professional porn types we see today. These were eight mm. no sound black and white films taken in Cuban or Mexican brothels. I was told that if I ever said any-thing I would 'git hurt...bad'... of course I said nothing...ever. They featured group sex, women having sex with dogs, women having sex with women, and every possible form of oral sex.

Things today that are taken for granted in porn videos. However, at that point in time it was a real eye opener... so to speak...especially for a seventeen plus year old. In the meantime my friends in the Navy Reserve were going on week-end cruises aboard a Destroyer Escort sailing to Guantanamo Bay Cuba. These were pre-Castro days so they had liberty in wild Havana.

After about two months of one evening a week we went to one week-end a month drills.

The porn nights were over.

"VeHorn, report to the C.O. on the double."

"Yes Sergeant, on the double"

"Yer in trouble now boy... hah... hah ...hah." Was all I heard as I shakily ran to the headquarters' office.

The air conditioned office felt cold after being in the sweltering heat of the huge armory drill hall. The headquarters' company master chief sergeant greeted me with a big smile...I thought that was odd... but I soon discovered why.

"When you go into the C.O.'s office stand at attention, salute and say private VeHorn reporting as ordered sir... got that?" he opened the C.O.'s door.

"At ease VeHorn... I went over your test scores and see that you not only knocked the top off the administrative section, but you make A's in English and you know how to type.. .I need a smart administrative clerk here in headquarters... this will be a permanent assignment and as soon as you memorize all the forms I'll promote you to private first class...report to the sergeant. .. dismissed." The C.O. was straight and to the point.

"Yes sir," I said as I did an about face and left his office.

"You got that VeHorn?...from now on you are assigned to the headquarters company and you report directly to me... as soon as you prove to me that you have memorized all the forms you will be promoted to private first class... and from now on you don't wear fatigues... you wear class A uniforms." The Sergeant was ecstatic

So that was it... the sergeant wanted someone else to handle the hated paper work. That was fine with me, and within one month I had all the forms down cold. No one could believe that I actually had my first stripe and hadn' t even been to basic training. The published orders came out on the Company bulletin board stating that my time in ROTC qualified me to be PFC... necessity is definitely the mother of invention.

My senior year was drawing to a close and my senior thesis in English was coming due. I was determined that to write a meaningful fully referenced thesis and not just some typical trivial high school cookie cutter drivel... and did I ever. My intent was to create a study not only worthy of publication... somewhere….but to send it to college admission directors as well. Unfortunately, my thesis cost me dearly.

Somehow I just didn't get it that any educated person, like a teacher, would be biased. A type of hidden prejudice was something I wasn't really aware of at that time. I submitted my paper entitled "Black and White and Hate All Over." The entire next chapter is that thesis. I received a flat "F" for my efforts. A year later I showed this to one of my college English instructors who verified this to be an A thesis. She said the grade was politically and racially motivated.

The price I paid included not only the "F" grade which resulted in a lowering of my grade point average, but the loss of the lead part in the senior play. Unfairly, it didn't stop at the school house door.

The week end following that shocker I had a National Guard drill. I went into the headquarters office and sat at my desk to work.

"VeHom, report to the motor pool." The sergeant barked.

"Right sergeant." I said as I walked to the motor pool in my class 'A' uniform thinking that I was going to pick up some reports.

"VeHorn put those rubber gloves on and pull all the batteries out of the jeeps and three quarter ton trucks... and clean the battery terminals." The sergeant of the motor pool smirked.

The motor pool specialist told me we had to finish all of them by tonight no matter how long it takes... and of course put them all back in. Two of the motor pool privates worked with us. We all had goggles on to keep battery acid from getting into our eyes. They all had rubber aprons on over their fatigues. The specialist said they had others but they were in the ambulances which had left for training in the morning. By ten P.M. we were finished and exhausted. The pants of my class A uniform and my T-shirt were a mass of holes and stains. Fortunately I had taken off my shirt. The specialist was from Chicago and we were both Cubs fans. He pulled me off to the side.

"Hey kid, you didn't hear it from me... all I can say is watch what you write... you know these crackers are still fight' n the Civil War."

OK so I paid the price... twice... once at school and once at the Guard. What a learning experience this whole fiasco had been. I learned that you can be right but still pay the price. The next day was Sunday. I reported to my desk at the headquarters' company office in my class A uniform, new pants and freshly polished shoes. Not a word was said about the day before. After all, the paper work had backed up and the sergeant was not about to do it.

CHAPTER 8 (OPTIONAL)

———◆———

CHAPTER EIGHT IS THE THESIS and bibliography. Keep in mind that this was written by an almost eighteen year old senior in high school who was witness to a time when America was in grave turmoil. This is a copy of the real thesis. I saved this for all of these years as a reminder of what bigotry can do. You may be surprised if you choose to read it.

However, after reading this... ask the question... how much has changed in fifty years?

"Black and White and Hate All Over"
Paul VeHom

Outline
I. WW II brought changes
    A. Integrated services and their results
    B. Integration of labor

II. Years from 1945-1950
    A. Active NAACP
    B. Communist infiltration of minority groups

III. 1951-1961 Integration years
    A. Southern resistance
        1. Little Rock "incident"
        2. " Integration"
        3. Resulting losses
        4. Lynchings
    B. NAACP
        1. Sit-ins
        2. Dr. Martin Luther King
    C. Federal Courts
        1. Constitution Amendments
        2. Civil Rights

BLACK AND WHITE AND HATE ALL OVER

IT IS MOST IMPORTANT TO have a clear and concise understanding of the problems of race relations in our democracy today.

The object of this manuscript is to give an unbiased illustration of race relations in America since WW II.

World War II brought many changes in America's race relations. During the war years from nineteen forty-one through nineteen forty-six the country as a whole, worked together. However the week of June twenty-first, nineteen forty-three completely contradicts the previous sentence. It was during this week that thirty-four Americans died as a result of a race riot in Detroit, Michigan.[1] While the sons of these people in Detroit were shedding their blood for democracy, the people were involved in anti democracy demonstrations.

By surveying the problems and tensions of the Detroit riot we can use this as a key to unlock the problems of race relations in the last two decades. The problems of nineteen forty-three are same as those of today.

---

(1) Lee and Humphrey, "Race Riot" (New York, 1943), pp. 2-4

The Negro in the armed services enjoyed much more freedom than he did at home. Thus, after his discharge he felt, and rightly so, that he deserved as much as the next fellow.

The white soldier began to accept the Negro more, due to his association with him.[2] There were two factions of white service men. One was the southern ' die hard' and the other the northern 'neutral'. The 'die hard', needless to say, was against the Negro in most cases, while the neutral simply didn't care.

Thus we have the following three types of citizens in our country at the end of WW II: the ' freed' Negro, the ' neutral northerner, and the ' die hard' southerner. All Three of these men came back to the States with one idea in mind and that was to get home and make money, all except the Negro. In his plans were the ideas of leaving his exploited condition whether it was in the south or north and then to seek a better livelihood.

The country had an all time high economic condition in nineteen forty-six. Trade unions as well as industrial unions were accepting anyone and everyone into their working force. This included the Negro.[3]

With everyone working the situation in nineteen forty-six looked promising. The slum areas which accounted for much of the strife and rioting in Detroit were being changed or greatly improved. The recreation areas, too, were far more numerous.

Everything had changed. That 'everything' included man's reasoning. The southern Negro, out of fear, was given more suppression. The northern Negro wanted more freedom. Out of pity he was

---

(2) Ibid., pp. 14-16

(3) Aliene Austin, ' The Labor Story' (Toronto, 1949), pp.104-197.

given more freedom. Since both factions wanted more freedom they searched for a way to have it.[4]

As a result for this want for 'freedom' or, to go a step further, a want for deserved rights, organizations were introduced to hold high the Negro banner. Such names as the Urban League and the Colored Man's Club sprang up along with the older and more progressive NAACP.[5] to see that the Negro was justly dealt with. As a still final result, the smaller organizations merged with the NAACP to form a mighty back-bone to counter-act Negro exploitation.

The NAACP was accused of being everything from black supremacists to subversives. It is unfortunate that such a group be blamed for being subversive. However, it is tragic when this group is justly accused.[6]

After a three day public hearing period, the investigating committee definitely proved there was Communist influence in the Little Rock School integration dispute. Manning Johnson, a former party member, testified that the crises had been investigated by the NAACP backed by the Communist party.[7]

One could name the period from nineteen fifty through nineteen sixty-one as the integration years. Despite the resistance and badgering, complete integration is inevitable. Southern as well as northern resistance is to no avail. The resistance to integration in the south far surpasses that in the north. The Little Rock, Arkansas school integration policy illustrates this fact. Racial violence hit an all time high during this period of integration.

---

(4) Ina Brown, ' Race Relations in a Democracy' (New York, 1949), pp.136-140.

(5) 'NAACP 'Universal Standard Encyclopedia (New York, 1957), pp. 5992-5993.

(6) 'Communists in U.S. Integration.' 1960 World Almanac (New York, 1960), p. 87

(7)

Arthur S. Fleming, Secretary of Health, Education and Welfare, deplored the closing of thirteen schools in Little Rock, Arkansas and Virginia to avoid racial integration.

Improvised schools were insufficient and three thousand, four hundred students received absolutely no schooling whatsoever when public schools were closed.[8]

The stubborn resistance hindered the negro as well as the white. In further defiance, Governor Lindsay Almend, Jr.'s only comment was, "... strictly Federal, NAACP propaganda".[9] This statement made by Governor Almend Jr. typifies the belligerent attitude taken by the southern people in general. There is nothing to be gained from opposing another race, creed or religion.

The losses resulting from race disruption ranges from economic ruin to moral chaos. Referring to the Detroit race riot let us examine each loss step by step.[10]

The first loss may be classified as individual insecurity. An expression of fear and distrust of a member of another race were Hitler's chief weapons for world domination. This tension and distrust can ruin human understanding and build up barriers that could halt the advancement of democracy. This basic drive of distrust may lead to an entire population with unhealthy mental attitudes. A type of 'social distance' is achieved when hypocritical statements such as these are made: "One of my best friends is a Negro", or "I employ many Negros". When a riot takes place individual insecurity mounts and snowballs. The consequence of a riot remains and festers deeply.

---

(8)
(9)
(10)

The second loss may be called a social paralysis. This is a different type of loss, but it must be considered. In dealing with both races the society or government must exercise the most conservative policies so as not to cause more dispute by giving one side more.

The most conservative policies were set so as not to cause more dispute by giving one side more than the other. Thus, public facilities are not able to operate at their highest level and must in effect, remain ' frozen'.

The third loss is very dangerous. We cannot forget that America is the backbone of democracy. It is America that shouts, ' Freedom for All', and yet in its own backyard riots against minorities are taking place. The eyes of the world are not closed to the fact we have these racial disorders. Thus the third loss is the degradation of democracy.

The aforementioned losses are more than losses; they are 'wounds' to society. There are but three 'wounds' that are not so obvious. The losses that are most outstanding will now be shown.

Counted as number four on our loss list is that of a danger to democracy. It has been said that democracy is more than a way of life; it is almost a religion. This is based on the fact that Christianity was the forerunner of democracy. The very nature and substance of democracy is endangered by race riots. This fourth group of consequences of race riots represents the really fundamental problem. [11]

The way to cure such wounds to society is to use every means at our disposal to make sure that democracy is given a better and better chance to function and thus prove itself. [12]

---

(11) Joe. c it.
(12) loc. cit.

The last and final loss in our list of consequences may be termed as personal and public property loss. This loss is to be considered insignificant as compared with the previously mentioned problems and results.

By examining what happened in nineteen forty-three, we can determine what would happen today if the same situation were present. It is wise to remember the past as a basis for the future.

Now let us refer back to the integration years, that period of time when minority groups became bolder. Lynching is a term applied when one or a group of individuals dole out punishment without due process of law. Since nineteen hundred, one thousand nine hundred and ninety Americans have been lynched. This is appalling. We may ask ourselves the following question. "How can Americans, a democratic people do a thing like this?' The 'how' we do not know, but the ' whom' we do know. Out of this frightening number of persons lynched, all but one hundred ninety five of them were colored. [13] This means that one thousand seven hundred ninety five of them were Negroes. This finger of guilt rests heavily on upon the 'Jim Crow' insurrectionists of the southern United States. Such action is terrible and brings nothing but hate and bitterness. Perhaps it is such events which cause race riots. Although lynchings are declining in number, the problem still exists in the United States today. [14]

When a minority group is exploited it usually bands together to form an organization for its protection. Although the NAACP has been mentioned before, it is important to now go through its many phases in order to have a clearer understanding of the material to follow.

_____

(13) " Lynchings". 1960 World Almanac (New York, 1960), p. 310

(14) Ibid.

[15]The NAACP was founded in nineteen ten for purposes of aiding minority groups, be they Negro or not. The opposition to this organization was so intense that that it became popular almost 'overnight'. Ironically the organizations greatest opposition, the southern bloc states, was to be its greatest friend.[16] Minority groups in any society become fertile soil for the seeds of subversiveness to thrive.[17] However, the NAACP has never had affiliations with any subversive group until recently. This recent development is not as bad as it may seem. The subversive group that became identified with the NAACP during the Little Rock incident was of communist root. The reason that this development is not so serious is that an organization of this nature cannot function properly and may defeat its own purpose by becoming connected with a subversive type of group.

[18]To prove that the Negro is a minority group, out of a hundred seventy-four million population (recorded in July, nineteen fifty-eight) only eighteen million are Negro. The Negro in the United States before the founding of the NAACP remained in the south until around eighteen eighty. At this time they began to migrate north very slowly. They were hired immediately in most cases due to personnel shortages in the north. Thus with the Negro in the north, the NAACP, or a group like it was an inevitable consequence.

[19]By nineteen twenty-nine, Negroes became an integral part of labor. They were mostly of the unskilled variety and the small per-

---

(15) loc. cit.

(16) Ibid., p.310

(17) loc. cit.

(18) 'U.S Population.' 1960 World Almanac (New York, 1960), p. 262

(19) 'Negros in the U.S. Universal Encyclopedia (New York, 1957), pp. 6045-6048

centages of skilled Negro workers were not recognized by the AFL. They were forced to form their own unions. The AFL held many anti-negro prejudices at this time. The Negro became known as a 'scab' in labor circles since he was a strike breaker. However in nineteen thirty, the Negro was given a break in the labor field. Due to efforts made by the NAACP, the CIO admitted large masses of Negro workers into their labor unions on a complete 'equality' with white workers.[20] Thus the NAACP has done a great deal to further the right of Negros. The effectiveness of the NAACP has been shown by various examples. We now will take a look at the methods used by this organization and its present day leader. Methods of obtaining rights have varied from boycotts to forceful integration. A new tactic which has been employed is that of 'sit-in' demonstrations. The only bad feature of using such methods is that by trying to obtain justly deserved rights there is a tendency to infringe upon the rights of others. It is the old question of, do the means justify the end. To this question a definite no must be answered. However, where the rights of one individual is lacking in a democracy, the rights of all individuals in that society are in jeopardy.

The 'sit-in' demonstrations may take place at any segregated ' public' service. These 'public' services may be in the form of a theatre, a restaurant, or any number of entertainment facilities. To sit-in simply means what it says and that is to enter a place of business and to stay until served. When a group of Negros enter an establishment and do not get served, it may look at first as though they lost this round but in reality they have won. The publicity will be broadcast across the nation almost as soon as the action is committed.

---

(20) Ibid.

[21]The true 'martyr' of the ' sit-ins' is one Dr. Martin Luther King. He is an educated Negro with a Ph.D. in theology. He has headed the 'sit-ins' and was leader of the Montgomery, Alabama bus boycott in nineteen fifty-four. This Negro leader has suffered jail sentences and physical harm at the hands of 'die-hard' segregationists in the south. Dr. King is confident that his efforts will result in complete and final integration.

What does the Federal Government have to say about the integration-segregation problem? The voice of our Constitution is echoed in today's courts. "We the people of the United States, etc...believe that all men are created free and equal before God their maker..."

[22] The Bill of Rights (Equal Rights law section) makes the following two points very clear.

1. The right of the citizens of the United States to vote shall not be abridged or denied by the United States or any state on account of race, color, previous condition of servitude.
2. The Congress shall have power to enforce this article by appropriate legislation.

This is the picture of race relations in our democracy. Whether white or black we are all people. Unfortunately, the problem isn' t that simple and only much thought and prayer will solve this issue. The problem lies in the hearts of man.

---

(21)

(22) "Equal Rights Law" 1960 World Almanac (New York, 1960), p.622

BIBLIOGRAPHY

———◆———

Almanac, World. New York: World Telegram, 1960

Austin, Aliene. The Labor Story. Toronto: Green and Company, 1949

Brown, Ina. Race Relations In A Democracy. New York: Harper and Brothers Publishers, 1949

Funk and Wagnalls. Universal Standard Encyclopedia. New York: Standard Reference Works, 1957

Lee and Humphrey. Race Riot. New York: Dryden Press, 1943

Life. Chicago: Time Inc.,1960. November 7.

Life. Chicago: Time Inc. 1960. November 28.

———————◆———————

CHAPTER 9

My DAD AND MOM FOR whatever reason were divorced. My mom was his first wife out of seven. Dad was male model handsome, and women loved him. I think it was more than this...I truly believe that an essence of male hormones were constantly effervescing from his body. It seemed that women would follow the trail of his scent to meet him. He was one of those few lucky men who was in fact a female magnet.

Dad was a disabled Navy Vet and was hospitalized at the Naval base in San Diego where he met his second wife. Divorces are never amicable no matter how many people say otherwise. He failed to pay full child support to my mother although he could easily afford it. I was his only offspring and I felt that mom deserved better. .. so... during my first year in college I sued him for the balance and I won. He had the temerity to fight it, but mom received the money plus interest. He really respected me after that for "having the balls" to fight him as he put it.

Dad was a highly successful business owner in Hayward, California and had contracts with the USAF for power spray equipment. He was a devout Democrat and had no use for Ronald Reagan as Governor and certainly not as President. He blamed the GOP for cut backs in veteran benefits, and of course he was right. He would often say the GOP meant Greed Over People. Just to hear him rant I called him one day after Reagan as President had given a speech... I expected dad to have something profound to say about it... did he ever.

"Hi dad how is it going?"

This happened at a later time after I was married the first time and had offspring.

"A-OK son, how is it with the family?"

"Great... we're coming out there soon."

I was now in the Navy Reserve as a Naval Instructor. Enlisting in the Navy put me back into my dad's good graces. He was right in wanting me to be in the Navy before.

Sometimes kids don't listen and pay the price as a result. I served with guys who were professional in their jobs and had a sense of duty. I was always proud to serve in the Naval Reserve.

Then I popped the question. Having been around Navy and Marine personnel, I thought I had heard every expletive in the English language in every possible combination...but the one I was about to hear from my dad erupted from the bowels of the contempt he felt for Reagan in particular and the GOP in general. In fact it was so good that I shared it at the next Reserve meeting with the Marine gunny sergeants.

"Dad did you just hear President Reagan's speech?"

"Let me tell you something son, if l want to hear from an asshole I'll fart!"

Thus ended the gospel according to my dad.

For my eighteenth birthday my dad flew me out to California during Spring break. Life was wild and crazy during that time in the San Francisco Bay Area. His exclusive home was located in the rolling hills near the Berkley campus. The pool overlooked San Francisco Bay... the sunsets were spectacular.

On my second day there I got up at around eleven A.M. I put on my bathing suit and strolled out to the kitchen. When the smell of freshly brewed coffee opened my eyes...that wasn't all that opened my eyes.

"Ah... good morning... who are you?

From the bottom up I could see high heel shoes designed for pool use with perfectly painted toes in a shade that perfectly matched her tawny Asian toned complexion... her slender legs stretched up to her black bikini bottom which was attached by two bow strings on either side of her slim hips... up further still was the black bikini top with a bow in the back that encased an "A" cup that hardly contained its contents... even the black shade of the bikini top could not mask the distinct shape of the protruding nipples underneath... up further still was dark highlighted wavy Farah Fawcett styled hair....her emerald green Asian shaped eyes flashed as her smile started to speak.

"My name is Lana...I' m your dad's friend."

"uh... hi Lana... nice to meet you."

"You're going to be stuck with me today... your dad won't be home until late."

I should be so lucky... I thought... I would like to stick her. I better cool it this could be a problem.

"Do you go to school at Berkley?"

"Well yes and no, I am a teaching assistant working on my masters, I ought to be done this year. I understand you are graduating from high school in June?"

"Yeah, thank god, finally."

"Let me put a cover on and we'll sit by the pool have some coffee and get acquainted"

As she walked past toward the bedroom the scent of her perfume wafted by me...I watched each of her steps as her body swayed toward the bedroom. I was getting turned on and I had on a tight bathing suit. I wish I had worn my trunks... or maybe not. She didn't really have to put on a cover for me.

When she entered from the bedroom her bikini was now even more provocative since her "cover" was black sheer... thigh length... and open.

She handed the coffee mug to me...her fingers were perfectly manicured and her nail polish matched that on her toes. What a class act I thought... but of course with my dad it was always the best or nothing.

"Let me hold your coffee while you sit down," She said.

With that she bent over to hand the coffee mug to me. Her bikini top drooped down and I could see her very large nipples that were protruding while trying to hide under the black "A" cups. They stuck out like thumbs... and I was instantly turned on. She must have known I thought.

"OK, you hold my mug while I sit down," she smiled.

Again, she leaned over and this time her right nipple was fully open as she took the mug and somewhat tried to tug the right top up. She smiled again and leaned back looking at me. I had to say something.

"uh... are you from California?"

Not the smoothest line in the world nor was it said in a debonair manner. I felt awkward... but she made me feel at ease in spite of the rise in my bathing suit... which I know she could see since she was looking right at it.

"I was born in California, but my dad is British and my mother is Chinese. My mother was pregnant when they got here and I was a sudden citizen. My dad was in the diplomatic corp. so I am a British citizen too."

"It's really too chilly to sit out at the pool let's just sit in the family room." She said as she took my hand and led me in to the family room/den.

Through the huge slightly tinted sliding glass doors the romantic view was pure Hayward Hills California. Stunning sunsets across the bay were reflected in the San Mateo Bridge. The cool blue swimming pool patio backed up to the sliding glass doors. Inside, a burning fireplace to the right of the glass doors was warming the morning. Across the room an oversized L shaped couch group faced the doors and fireplace. A chaise lounge sat to the right facing the couch group. Now visualize the layout... oh yeah, right in front of the seating was a low coffee table.

"Lay back on the chaise, I'll bring in rolls and fresh coffee." Lana's voice was trialing to the kitchen.

" You' re going to love these rolls... Maui Wowie... and warm too."

I must have looked puzzled.

"Maui Wowie is probably the best pot around," she laughed.

" Lana, I have never had pot before...remember I live in what is still the South... those anal retentive cracker politicians still have counties where you can't buy alcohol."

The warm cinnamon buns were of the pop open the package variety with what looked to be parsley sprinkled over the top. The same "parsley" was wedged inside the cinnamon swirls. They tasted like regular buns.

Lana curled up on the couch in front of the coffee table while I was on the chaise next to her. I began to feel really different. .. not drunk but really good and really aware.

" Hey these really taste good." I heard myself saying.

"If you think they Taste good now just wait." She laughed.

We both became quiet and Lana looked at me intensely... my cock was beginning to strain in my bathing suit... Lana got up made two steps and dropped to her knees in front of me on the chaise lounge. She looked up at me as she slowly moved the palms of her hands up my inner thighs and then around to the sides of my bathing suit and she smoothly slid my bathing suit down... across my knees and down to the floor. I could feel her hair touch both sides of my legs as she moved her head up between them. My cock started to throb as she slowly moved her wet tongue from the base of my balls to that sensitive spot right under my now purplish penis head.

"Oooo you have a huge head...just like your dad's," she said as she slipped her hot lips over my head and down the shaft.

I had to really hold back because I knew the best was yet to come... if I did not cum first. She must have known that would happen. Lana then stood up and slowly took off her top...her pointed nipples jutted out over an inch. The areola was the puffy type. It was all I could do to keep from exploding. She then untied the sides of her bikini bottoms. As they dropped to the floor I saw what I had never seen in girls from high school... a completely shaved Mons... an erotic masterpiece. I never again wanted anything but a smooth quim. Under the influence of the Maui Wowie everything seemed slower and in HD. Lana's vaginal lips stuck out just slightly... they were wet and glistening. She straddled the chaise lounge as she moved her body closer to my face. I began to realize that I was her student. My face was now so close that my nostrils were filled with her musky sex scent. Everything seemed as if it were in slow motion. She then held my head on either side with her hands.

"I'm going to teach you how to really turn a woman on... very lightly and slowly move your tongue up one side of my lips and then up the other...that's right...don't rush.. .ooo that's good.. .now take both hands and slightly open my lips...dart your tongue lightly on my clit... that little crown you see on top... again...again...keep going... keep going...now slip your tongue inside...harder... harder," with that she pushed my face into her wet hot twat.

Lana shuddered and then let out a loud squeal...she was not only wet, but a clear sweet liquid squirted out...I thought it was pee but it wasn't...some women ejaculate...and that's what it was. I licked up every possible drop the taste was delicious especially under the pot influence. She then stepped backwards and straddled me over my hard throbbing cock...she still had her heels on which gave her more leverage...as she placed my cock head into her Mons she let out a moan.

"Owww big head ... don't do anything... I'll make the moves," she said in a husky voice.

Her skin tone glowed as she moved my shaft in and all the way out and in again... until finally when I was all the way in I grabbed her hips and held her down on as my hard ridged rod exploded... finally...I heard myself screaming in the background and I heard her shrieking...as we both came together...Then we both collapsed.

We woke up on the couch together. We talked... mostly she talked and I listened...I really was getting an education. Her heels were still on and she had a kimono snugly tied around her. She had thrown a blanket over me while I was asleep.

"Did you know that the Egyptians invented high heels...they had public baths and they knew that a woman looked better when her derriere was elevated and her legs looked longer...so they would step into their wood high heels and look chic...I really don't get it...why do American women take off their heels when they make love," she said in a rather condescending tone.

"After being with you today, I don't ever want them to take their heels off... ever."

"There is a British joke which goes, good girls wear heels to church...bad girls wear heels to bed," she laughed.

I remember that one and I totally agree. When I have told that to women most agree. Lana went on about my sexual education... how women in Europe always wear something while having sex since only animals have sex with nothing on.

"I have always been turned on by women who wear nylons and gar-ter belts or at least thigh highs or open crotch panty hose... they should keep them on during sex...and I never want to see another woman who doesn't shave herself... that is really hot... you ruined me," I said.

Lana laughed, "Good, I'm glad... you're becoming more sophisti-cated... and women love that... at least the ones that you' re going to want...you could have it all... you should have it all."

CHAPTER 10

———◆———

THAT EVENING DAD CAME HOME from his business with a complete Chinese dinner in tow. We used the coffee table for dinner and sat on big pillows. Lana was in the middle and we sat on either side. The sunset was a study in art...the orange, pink, and purple hues reflected across the bay. The dinner conversation was small talk about Chinese vs. Thai vs. Polynesian cuisine. Lana wore a modest black skirt with nylons and heels on of course. She and I quickly cleaned the coffee table. Dad brought in two bottles of chilled Champagne, popped the corks and poured the Champagne into black and white crystal Champagne flutes. I sat on the chaise lounge while dad and Lana were cuddled together on the couch. Among other toasts we finally toasted to my 18th birthday.

"Well how did you like your birthday present son?" he laughed.

They both laughed, but I didn't get it. I didn't receive anything from him. I thought he meant the trip out here so I responded.

"Yeah, thanks dad I really am having a swell time out here... I never flew that far in a plane before... you have a great place... your home is really cool. .. I liked seeing your business too." I was totally oblivious.

Then I thought uh oh he knows about me and Lana... I am in some deep soup now... I became really nervous... they could see that I was uncomfortable ... but they were both laughing.

" I don't mean coming out here... Lana was your birthday present... unless you wanted something wrapped up with a ribbon on it," he laughed so hard tears rolled down his cheeks.

They were both laughing and my face was turning red.

"Well how did he do Lana... is he a good student?" he asked still laughing.

"He did really well, but he is still a work in progress... we will have to have to have some homework," she said still laughing.

Sadly, the day had come for me to leave, but the morning brightened when Lana rushed into the kitchen wearing a bright orange dress.

"Son, it has been a trip having you here for a few days.. .love to have you come out any time... maybe go to college at Berkley... Lana will take you to the airport the long way over the Golden Gate bridge... Lana take the caddy... Paul I'm sure you'll never forget the Golden Gate Bridge," he laughed.

With that we said our good byes and Dad left the house for work. I wouldn't see him again for several years. It always seems that time has a way of leaving before we want it to. That's why my dad would say: life leaves us before we are ready to leave life. He decided to live life to the fullest since life nearly left him in the service.

"Here catch... you drive," Lana said tossing the caddy keys to me.

I thought she was really cool to let me drive the caddy. This was a four door sedan which had bench style seats in both the front and back with a fold down arm rest... at that time only the two door model had bucket seats.

We drove north on 880 and crossed San Francisco Bay at East Richmond. The bright morning sun painted red streaks across the blue sky as it cleared the fog. During the trip Lana talked about my dad, where they traveled, and what a sexually exciting relationship they had.

"Okay now, listen to me hon.. .I want you to keep your eyes on the road, get into the right lane and concentrate only on driving... no matter what," Lana smiled.

As I drove on to the bridge Lana put a tape into the deck. Suddenly Richard Wagner ' s "Ride of the Valkyries" boomed... high volume.. .intense. My senses were alert... adrenalin was pumping... sexcitement was in play. Lana moved the armrest up and placed her head in my lap as she unzipped my pants. Her hand was around my cock shaft. The Valkyries were charging through my mind.

"Don't let go till you get to the center of the bridge... just hold on," Lana commanded.

As her mouth slipped over the head of my throbbing cock it was all I could do to concentrate on driving. Her left hand was slightly squeezing and releasing as she slid it up and down over my cock. All the while her brightly painted finger nails of her right hand offered an ever so light pain as she scratched my testicles. Lana then started to flick her tongue on that super sensitive point right under the head while her mouth was still completely over the head.

" Aaaaaaahhh," I let out a scream as I felt a huge amount of sperm pump into her mouth. "Oh my god I love how you taste... just like your dad," she said.

Lana licked her lips and my cock leaving no sperm that might have been left. Lana gently put my cock back into my pants and zipped it up. She then sipped some orange juice we had picked up earlier. I was completely drained, but still driving. She turned off the Valkyries. Although they may not know it that was the wildest ride the Valkyries ever had.

"So this was planned ahead by you and dad?"

"Of course... you don't think I would do anything without his okay do you... Follow the signs to North Beach... I'll drive from there hon." She smiled.

"Oh is it my turn then while you are driving?" I laughed.

"Great idea, but I have to go to class this afternoon and I don't need to decorate my dress."

We got to North Beach and stopped at a gift shop. Lana bought a poster of The Golden Gate Bridge for me. It still is one of my favorites. I can never see a picture of The Golden Gate Bridge or hear Richard Wagner's "Ride of the Valkyries" without remembering. We said our farewells... Lana dropped me at the airport.. .I never saw her again. She was one of those incredible experiences in life that modifies your behavior forever. From then on sex became far more sensual... there had to be something interesting... different...

erotic... for me to be really interested in seducing a woman... of course if a woman chose to seduce me she would have to have at least some redeeming social value... and class.

The return flight was filled with angst and soul searching My values had been challenged and my life had changed. I saw the future and I knew...my life could be amazing.

CHAPTER 11

———◆———

FROM THE SUBLIME TO THE ridiculous I thought as the troop train was pulling out of a main station on Florida' s West Coast. My mother was very upset. The last thing she wanted was for me to be in the Army. She even wanted me to join the regular Navy before leaving for six months of active Army duty since she and my dad were both in the Navy he was regular and she was civilian Navel personnel. Then you could join a regular active branch from the reserves at any time.

As the train meandered through Florida it stopped at every crossing to pick up draftees, regulars, reservists, and yes even Army National Guard recruits. From Florida's West Coast to Orlando to Jacksonville. We then went to Pensacola, Mobile, New Orleans, Birmingham, and Atlanta and finally to Columbia, but not before we went to dozens of stops in between. For two and a half days we were never off the train.

Thankfully I had my own compartment with wash basin, swing down cot, fresh sheets and towels. However at times I would go out into the regular train cars and sit with the other recruits. Maybe because I talked with the black conductor about a book I was reading that I carried on to the train, Carl Sandburg's Lincoln, that he assigned me to a compartment. He assigned compartments and I later found out that they were reserved for recruits going to OCS (Officer Candidate School).

The conductor was pretty sharp. When he had some downtime we would talk in my compartment. He was from Chicago and went to college for a year before he got a job on the railroad. He was in his forties and served in WWII on the red ball express which he described as a continuous truck convoy in Europe carrying supplies to the front. He was a driver but they also had to load the trucks. He told me that the red ball express drivers were primarily black.

"Young man you're going to have a tough time with these southern boys cause you're a Yankee... just because you happen to be from Florida doesn't mean a thing cause you're still a Yankee." He said as he shook his head.

He was right on. Maybe getting the compartment had something to do with that. I understand that fights did break out on the train but I didn't see any of them. MPs (Military Police) on board kept order. Whenever they would break up a fight the MPs would make sure that the recruit's faces showed it so that others would understand that it was a bad idea to fight.

"On your feet... grab your gear... fall out on the platform," a big burley black sergeant bellowed.

"Who told you to talk trainee... get down and give me twenty pushups," he growled.

Having been in ROTC I knew the best idea was to keep your mouth shut. The "boot" (trainee) couldn't do twenty. A new sergeant ran up... one of those real mean skinny type guys with a gravelly voice... a combat infantry man' s insignia on his uniform and an Army Airborne patch... he had a glass eye... obviously not a guy to cross.

"What's your name boy?" he screamed as the heavy set trainee struggled to do one more pushup but couldn't get up off his stomach."

The next part was just too good.. .his answer could have been right out of "Saturday Night Live" only there was no "Saturday Night Live" at that time. There were hundreds of guys on the platform... not one word... but his answer brought smirks and closed eyes to the rest of the guys... all but laughter...by this time they knew better.

"Thaddeus Beauregard sir," he said as by now he lay face down on the platform. It was later I found out that his middle initial was "T"...That would be Thaddeus T. Beauregard apparently the name of a famous Confederate States of America general who was also known as "Napoleon" for a nickname... at least that' s what this kid said. He claimed he was related to the General. Talk about bad luck... this kid finally was in this sergeant's platoon for the full nine weeks of basic training...stay tuned... this sergeant actually sent him to outer space.

"Jesus Christ," was all the sergeant could come up with but he did add the F bomb between J. and C.

"Do I look like a sir to you boy?" I aint no god damned officer.

The next part was even better. The kid was obviously not the sharpest knife in the cutlery drawer... so his reply was a loud... no sir... it was all I could do to keep from laughing.

" Git off yer ass and on yer feet boy," This time in a low but loud voice, "I'm gonna run that fat offa you boy and if I don't run it off you I'm gonna fuck it off you... now git back in line."

On the way to the basic training company complexes trucks full of guys who had finished basic were being trucked out. They were all laughing, giving us fingers and saying..."you'll be sorry"...At that point I had no idea how right they were. "Un ass those trucks," all the sergeants were screaming.

The next scene became another unforgettable moment. All of the NCOs (non commissioned officers) were Army Airborne person-nel. Their job was two fold... make basic infantry soldiers out of us and try to get any one or all of us to go regular Army (RA) and volunteer for Army Airborne. Each platoon sergeant addressed each platoon in front of the drab yellow barracks with the same speech. They knew we were all from the South although some of us were transplanted "Yankees." In our case only two....I was one and the other was white but had the features of a black person. He was from Maryland. All the recruits in my company were Army National Guard and all white. The cadre was white and black.

"NG (i.e. National Guard) means no fucking good," the sergeant yelled.

At that moment Thaddeus T. Beauregard got lucky. The focus was off of him for a moment and on to some wise ass who yelled at the sergeant... a very very bad move.

"Sergeant there ain't no F in National Guard!"

All Hell broke loose... the whole platoon was ordered to do fifty push ups... at that point in our training nobody did fifty...

I managed about thirty... all the while our sergeant and a corporal were screaming at us... we were also told we would be the last platoon in the company to go to the mess hall and the guy' s squad who said it would be the last squad... for a week. Needless to say that fool was assigned to KP (kitchen police) for a week by his squad leader... that was me. I was assigned as acting sergeant for my squad since I had ROTC and already attained the rank of Private First Class.

June, July and August in Columbia, South Carolina was one hell of an experience... especially Army Airborne basic training with full packs, weapon, forced marches day or night or both... extreme heat... and voracious insects. When things became especially miserable we were ordered to do double time and chant the following: " Gotta go gotta go all the way all the way... Airborne... Airborne... good... good... cold beer... cold beer... bad... bad... girls... girls... bad... bad... Airborne... Airborne... good... good... this would go on for miles. The rumor was that if these drill instructors could get a trainee to go regular Army Airborne during basic they would get a bonus. And the trainee?..he would get a two week leave and finish basic training including jump school. Nothing could be better than that. I did not go that route. However, the best was yet to come.

That July day was so hot that you could fry an egg on your steel helmet. Some of the guys were dropping out from heat exhaustion, but that was ok because an ambulance was following our company to pick up the "wounded"... that would be "wounded" from heat exhaustion.

As for the subject of wounded I understand that the idiot secretary of defense Donald Rumsfeld had the word wounded changed to injured during the Iraq war because it was more palatable for the public to digest... of course the sheep-like media fell right into line and still use it. My combat veteran uncle said that when you have searing hot metal rip into your body you are wounded, but if you fall out of a tree you are injured. Of course if you fall on your head you may not know the difference. Is it true that "Rummy" was an inveterate tree climber?

Meanwhile, back at the hot July day, our buddy Thaddeus T. Beauregard was out of step even though we were at march step.

"God dammit Beauregard yer outa fuckin step... fall out boy...I told you I was gonna send your fat ass into outer space."

The sergeant was bellowing. All the while we kept moving in march step and so did Beauregard and the sergeant.

"You run in circles around this marching platoon at port arms and yell: I'm a sputnik, I'm a sputnik," the sergeant screamed.

I thought Beauregard was going to drop, but after about six rounds the sergeant halted the platoon and we fell out for a break. Ten minutes later, exactly, the break was over.

"Awright, off your asses and on your feet... saddle up... and Beauregard get back in the platoon and see if you can keep up boy." The sergeant barked.

Now the reason the Army Airborne cadre used the word boy on these southern all white National Guard guys is because they knew that the word "boy" was a demeaning term used in the south to address blacks. This same Army Airborne group had previously been sent into Little Rock, Arkansas to desegregate the schools. No love lost there. In fact the south was still resisting and the worst was going to happen within the year. Freedom riders, riots, and cross burnings were yet to come. America was going to face the most critical time in its history since the civil war.

Hypocrisy ran rampant. We had a black staff sergeant from New York City who was a combat vet. This guy was big... six foot four and a rock solid two hundred eighty pounds. Of course these weasely idiots didn't like him on two counts. First, he was black and second, he was from New York City. We had other black cadre but he was their black "Damned Yankee" of choice. I was called a "Damned Yankee" too, but I couldn't have cared less...I just considered the source... and besides I was an acting sergeant and could put them on report for guard duty, KP, or any other job like washing garbage cans. These nauseating weasels were very nice to his face but behind his back they called him "The New York (N word)."

Remember the guy from Maryland who was white but had black facial features? Well these low grade morons decided that he was a "White (N word)." That sounded like an oxymoron to me but what did I know. Looking back, I can only quote Lewis Black, " it boggles the mind." It was a dark and stormy night...I always wanted to write that (thank you Snoopy)... and it really was, plus we were on a forced night march. It was obvious that there were some towns in the south that were missing their village idiots because these schmucks decided it was the perfect time to beat the hell out of the " White (N word)." I saw two of them (the ring leaders) jump him and knock him to the ground.

They literally ambushed him. The column of men stopped moving...I kicked one of the perps with my size twelve boot right square in the ass...I slammed the other fool on the side of his helmet with my rifle. Fortunately, their favorite black "Damned Yankee" came down to break it up. The next part was pure righteousness.

"Look out, here come da "New York (N word)," in a mocking way to sound as if a black person might have said it, and loud enough to be heard by the staff sergeant.

"Acting sergeant VeHom, what the fuck is going on here?" he said it in a low angry voice.

He knew exactly what was going on, and he clearly had heard the pejorative statement. This time there was no screaming or yelling. By this time our platoon sergeant, the skinny mean guy just doing his job the one who sent Beauregard into outer space had joined the black staff sergeant. He ordered our platoon to drop out of column and fall in to platoon formation. They pulled the two miscreants out of the platoon and radioed the MPs to pick them up. Suddenly these big brave bone heads looked really scared, and I just loved it.

The two imbeciles spent three days and three nights in the stockade. When they returned for reveille on Monday morning there were noticeable bruises on them as well as some facial swelling. My guess is that the MPs spread the word and of course the stockade was integrated. The dumbass duo also received thirty days of extra duty plus no passes for the remainder of their basic training...Four weeks of harassment.

Unfortunately they had not learned their lesson. Being stupid stubborn they decided that I was persona non grata. One late afternoon they told their ignoranus (i.e. ignorant anus) cronies to cover for them while they went to the second floor of the barracks as I was directing a detail for barracks clean up duty. Suddenly my detail was gone and these two dimwits grabbed me.. .one on either side each by one arm and one leg. They spread my legs and started running toward a barracks upright. I was yelling at them and twisted just in time, and I got one leg free. Thus saving the family jewels. People heard the commotion and were running up the barracks steps while these two dropped me on the floor and went running out of the upstairs fire escape.

My feeling about them can be epitomized by something a ninety four year old man once told me. I asked him how he managed to live so long. He said, "I just wanted to outlive all those no good rotten bastards I hated."

---•---

I NEVER DID GET TO Fort Monmouth New Jersey as promised by the Florida Army National Guard Sergeant who recruited me. Instead I was sent back the fort where I did my basic training. My assignment was to the PIO (Public Information Office) as "on the job training." There wasn't a thing that I could do about it.

The PIO office was complete. We published the weekly base paper, sent press releases to hometown papers, did an on base radio show, and even broadcast a closed circuit TV show. I was soon to find out that I would be assigned to the base newspaper. Ironically, my first assignment was to cover our baseball team.

"Hey, acting sergeant VeHorn, what are you doing in that class A uniform?" he laughed. It was the staff sergeant from New York City.

"I' m with the PIO office and I'm here to cover the game... how about if you give me an interview after the game... get a couple runs and I'll put your picture on the sport's page."

"You got it man!"

I didn't know when I first spoke with him, but he was a real hitter. He got two singles and a double. On the double he hit a man in. He got his interview and his photo.

That all happened on the first day. The PIO sergeant was a twenty year plus veteran master sergeant. He made a couple corrections but he said he liked my work.

As I walked into the office on the second day, I felt a pair of piercing black eyes track my every move. Her complexion was as cream white as her hair was raven dark. Even in uniform her curves seemed to move seductively. I was later to find out that her Russian ancestry gave her that not heavy, but very solid body. Her family was Jewish and left Odessa before the Nazi invasion. She did go to Fort Monmouth and held the rank of Warrant Officer. A Warrant Officer is a special rank that is neither enlisted nor full officer. The rank is typically awarded to personnel with technical expertise such as instructors, intelligence, public information (media), etc. Therefore as a Warrant Officer, Tech (pronounced Tek for Techiya) could freely date either enlisted or commissioned personnel. She seemed to glide as she moved toward me... thanks to her early ballet lessons.

"What is your name soldier?" She said in an obvious broadcast voice.

No one in the room spoke a word. Although she wasn't the officer in charge... she was in charge. I was later to find out that she selected who she was going to see personally. Both officers and enlisted men wanted to date her. I snapped to attention, I knew that you did not salute a Warrant Officer, but it was a good idea to come to attention for a sergeant up to a Warrant Officer.

"Private first class VeHom... ma'am." I replied in a sharp response.

"PFC VeHorn, come into my office," she said in an easier tone of voice.

"Yes ma'am."

As I followed her into her office, I noticed that her black military pump heels were just elevating her derriere enough to make it interesting. I found myself getting somewhat aroused...oops I thought... at that moment she abruptly turned around.. .I swear I thought she looked right at my crotch... a slight smile played across her lips.

"At ease VeHorn, (I wondered how she meant that) and close the door," she said with a smirk.

I did a smart about face and closed the office door... as I walked back I thought... whew at least my cock relaxed.

"Have a seat VeHorn, I saw your sports page article... good stuff... from now on you will report to me... you take that desk right outside my door... you will be my administrative assistant for as long as you're here... you will be on call twenty four hours a day and accompany me to any event where reporting has to be done. If it is a formal event an Army blue dress uniform will be provided for you... you will have a class A pass and will have no garrison duties... your garrison OIC (officer in charge) will receive these orders today... oh... and by the way anything and everything is confidential.. .you keep your mouth shut...I did some checking on you and I know that you can be very secretive and that is an absolute in this office including my business your business or our business...

we will have intelligence briefings from time to time so I will get at least a secret clearance for you... any questions?"

"No ma' am."

As she stood up and said, "Dismissed" a beautiful smile revealed her brilliantly white teeth surrounded by just perfectly drawn red lips. In that moment I knew that this thirty six year old beauty had erotic plans for us. I wondered what it was about me that seemed to be so interesting to Tech. I was only eighteen and as far as she knew I had no experience whatsoever except for maybe a few high school girls. Maybe that was it, no experience. Maybe she was going to "teach" me, and that was her turn on. In some odd way Lana sort of decided to "teach" me. I had a premonition that this was going to be another incredible chapter in my life. My thoughts went to Lana...I hope Tech also removes all hair from her eyebrows down.

About ten days went by, and I continued to write for the base paper. I was no longer doing sports; Tech had me doing human interest articles.

"VeHom, come in here," Tech called from her office.

"Yes ma' am."

"We are going into town after work... to do some shopping...I Need to have you get some civilian clothes... I'll drive us, and we'll get some pizza after that... I'll drive you back later...meet me at the car." That's all she said.

Tech was sitting in the car and had changed out of her uniform by the time I got there. I had never noticed a smell of perfume on her before...a very pungent musky scent filled the car. Since her hair was always tightly pulled up in the office it was nice to see her long raven hair falling over her shoulders. Tech' s black full pleated skirt had slid up slightly above her knees...each time she shifted her red Triumph TR 4A the edge of her thigh would show revealing a garter belt attached to her nylons. Her military issued black pump shoes had given way to higher black heels with a strap across the ankle...very chic. A long sleeved silky blouse was mostly covered by her matching black blazer. Tech's thirty four Bs jutted out from between the lapels. I was awe struck... and I was already turning on.

"Just remember Paul, anything and everything is top secret between us... don't even think about saying a word or I promise I will bring you up on charges and you will be remanded to the stockade.. .Is that crystal clear?" Tech asked in a stern, threatening way.

That was the first time she had called me Paul, and I was even more intrigued.

"Yes ma' am, totally clear...why would I open my mouth and spoil a perfectly good thing?" I asked.

"Exactly, and it will be a perfectly good thing...no one will ever ask you about me...they know better... and you call me Tech outside of duty hours or events...I will use your first name in the same way... ok Paul?" Tech questioned with that radiant smile of hers.

"Alright Tech, I agree, and I feel a little better now and not so uptight," saying that I smiled back at her.

"When I said that no one will ever question you about me I meant exactly that... I have certain information on a file of people that they would never want revealed... in addition, my dad has considerable financial and political clout... he owns an international fabric wholesale business in New York," she said in a matter of fact way.

Tech also let me know that her dad had set up a trust for her so money was not an issue. Her plan was to transfer to the USIA (United States Information Agency). She did exactly that and became one of the directors for RFE (Radio Free Europe).

As I opened the door to a very classy men's store off the university campus, Tech let me know that she was buying...period. A double breasted blue blazer with gold buttons... two pair of slacks... two oxford button down shirts... two ties... belts... socks... shoes and finally, non military underwear. I changed before we left. I remember being dressed like this and feeling like I was already in college.

"I' m going to teach you a lot of things including how to dress... you'll leave all of these clothes at my place...when you depart back to your unit you'll take them with you," she said huskily.

"Tech, I'm curious... why me?"

"You're different... you're an only child... mostly you attended private schools...you have a very high IQ... and besides I really like men with blonde hair and blue eyes," then she flashed a different look at me.

"How did you find out all that info?"

"Oh come on... remember the secret clearance...I got a copy."

I was in the process of being seduced, and at that time I really didn't realize it. It was already about nine in the evening as Tech pulled the Triumph into the parking lot of what looked like a club.

"This is a really hip jazz club with a British theme... do you like jazz Paul?"

"Yeah I really do, some guy in Intel (Intelligence) at the barracks played a new album he had called "Take Five.""

"Good, I know that album... its Dave Brubeck... I saw him in concert over at the university."

As we walked through the parking lot at the "Cock and Bull" pub, I could really check out her smooth flowing figure. The higher heels elevated her derriere far better than the Army pumps. The sounds of deep night jazz drifted out as we walked into the red hued light....smoky air gave a surrealistic image to the trio as they played.

"Wow, I love this place, and the sound is so cool."

After saying wow I decided to not use it again since it sounded too high schoolish... strange how clothes can affect your personal style I thought. This was my first venture into the world of jazz, a university setting and a sophisticated life style. My inside voice let me know that I had just found a part of who I am.

" Paul, I'm going to order for us... British style pizza with red wine... cabernet sauvignon...remember that because it's my favorite." She said as she touched my forearm.

I was beginning to listen to her as well as at her... although I didn't realize that concept until I was in college. She was taking control by buying and coordinating my clothing, ordering meals, and touching me. Tech really knew what she was doing.

The ride back to her place was mostly small talk.

"When we get back to my place you change back into your uniform, and I'll drive you back to base... when I leave the office tomorrow you wait an hour then take a cab to my place." Tech smiled as she said it.

Her apartment complex was in an upscale, gated community. She didn't say a word as I followed her to the door of her townhouse. As we entered, several black lights flipped on, and still saying nothing she lit a few candles. The scent of jasmine incense which she also lit filled the room.

I just stood there as she slipped off her jacket which landed on the love seat. Tech then stood in front of me and slid my jacket off. Suddenly her face was in mine with her hands around my head, as she brought her lips to mine. Tech's tongue began to slowly circle the inside of my lips. I could feel her mound pushing against my now tightly throbbing erect shaft. First the right hand and then the left slipped below my waist as they pulled my body into her. I moved my arms under hers and around her back pressing her firm orbs against my body.

Abruptly, Tech stepped back...I could see that slight smile of hers.

"Not tonight...tomorrow night...now go change into your uniform I'll drive you back."

"Oh my god... O.k. O.k." I said, I wasn't about to argue.

After I changed into my class A-s, I went back downstairs. There was a master bedroom and a smaller guest bedroom upstairs as well as an office/den downstairs. I noticed a cylinder lock was on the office /den. Tech had already changed into jeans a shirt and tennis shoes. I guessed that was not to tempt me further.

"Trust me, this will be the most bizarre week end of your life." She said as she was driving.

I slept soundly, but my first thought when I opened my eyes was the week end. The day would pass way too slowly. Tech was strictly business like at the PIO office, and sent me out on an assignment. That was probably a good idea since it kept my mind occupied.

I didn't eat dinner since she planned to order out. The cab smelled like smoke, but I couldn' t roll the window down because the wind was carrying the paper mill stink across the base. For some reason the title of Dickens's book "Great Expectations" kept coming to mind.. .mmmm... I wonder why. This taxi was going way too slow.. .even though he was driving over the speed limit. We arrived...finally.

As I was buzzed through the gate.. .l heard the sultry sound of her voice saying... come in the door is open. I walked through the open door and locked it behind me.

Gentle Japanese Koto music was playing from behind a setting of a low table with two cushions facing across from each other. Japanese dishes and Saki cups were bathed in an amber light of table candles and strip lighting from above. On one of the cushions was Tech with her raven hair trussed up Japanese style. I could see she was wearing formal thongs; a red kimono was wrapped around her body. Items undoubtedly bought while stationed in Japan. She stood up and bowed at the waist.

"Tech want the honorable Mister Paul to go second bedroom and put on Japanese garment." She said with a sly smile.

Upon entering the bedroom I saw a black kimono, formal thongs, and a black silk pair of men's briefs. These were not your typical briefs however. The front of the briefs had a large circular hole; just enough for both my cock and balls to stick out through...a snug fit but that was the idea. I went downstairs dressed in my newest high fashion.

Tech was on the cushion sitting on her knees.

"Mr. Paul...sit...Tech pour Saki."

I caught a glimpse of her left nipple... red and rigid...as she bent over to pour the very warm Saki. I'm sure she knew her kimono opened. That was fine with me..I was half turned on already. On a bed of steamed white rice the shrimp tempura was exquisite as were the succulent gingered veggies. Tech insisted... commanded ... that I eat with chopsticks. She showed me how and I learned quickly.

"It' s like riding a bicycle... once you know, you'll never forget."

She showed me how to really appreciate Saki... how to not ever let it boil and to deeply inhale the vapors before sipping. The Saki was taking its toll. She filled the large serving pot three times. I noticed that I was drinking cup after cup... she always kept my cup filled. I was certainly drinking more than she was. I had a pretty good buzz going when the conversation drifted to a new area.

"Paul, baby, do you know what B and D is?'

That was the first time she ever called me baby and I loved it.

"I think so, the B means bondage and the D means…and…uh."

"Discipline…" She finished my sentence.

"Do you trust me?"

"Yeah, Tech… so far." I answered her.

" I' m going into the den.. .I'll call you when I want you to come in… relax…it will be just a little while," she smiled.

With that she came around the low table and gave me a long warm open mouth kiss. I was really turned on at that point. As I waited, the Saki buzz was getting stronger. I was not feeling sick, but I was feeling good… no…wonderful.

"Turn off the lights out there and blow the candles out… baby… then come in and lock the door behind you."

I did as I was told. I opened the den door to a surprisingly large room with thick plush carpeting and a small stage with wood flooring. I went in. Black light filled the room and illuminated the black light posters of nude dominatrix mistresses on the walls. Low gothic music was playing. One white pin light was aimed down from the ceiling. A wall was filled with sex toys, whips, chains, handcuffs, dildos and other objects I couldn't even identify. That sensual musky perfume scent that Tech wears filled my nostrils. By this time just her scent turned me on. I heard her voice.

"Take off everything except the briefs… now," she ordered.

I took off the kimono and the formal thongs. By this time my cock was rock hard and sticking straight up through the circle of the black silk briefs... Tech suddenly appeared under the pin spotlight.

Spiked shiny high heel laced boots went up to the knees of her legs which were spread apart. A wide leather garter belt was attached to black fish net nylons. I could see that Tech's smoothly shaved quim was wet and glistening in the pin light. Her engorged clit pointed downward to vaginal lips that protruded like small wings. Red ridged nipples stuck out of a shiny leather open nipple bra. Black fingerless elbow length fishnet gloves held a long black flogger. Her hair was down over her shoulders with the Japanese combs on either side. Blood red lips and dark eye make-up reflected eerily in the pin light's glow.

"Get on your knees," she demanded.

By this time I was so stunned and turned on that I wanted to see what was going to happen next. Within six months my world was moving at warp speed. First it was Lana and now Tech. The sex gods have smiled on me from the time I was a child... and I am forever grateful.

As I got on my knees, Tech walked forward from the small hard-wood stage to the carpet where I was kneeling. Her Mons was so close to my face I could almost taste her scent.

"Pull open the wings of my cunt."

By this time I was ready to squirt, but I held on. As soon as I pulled the wings open, Tech quickly grabbed the back of my head and shoved my mouth right between the lips. The wetness tasted musky and sweet at the same time. She then grabbed my hair.

"Stick out your tongue and lick my clit."

I could feel my hair being pulled slightly up as I lapped inside her lips and over the clit with my tongue.

"Faster…don't stop… don't stop…don't stop."

She started a low moan and it became louder until she had a climax so hard that liquid flowed out into my mouth and down the inside of her thighs. At that point she dropped the flogger and held my head in both of her hands while she pushed my face harder between her wet flowing winged lips. She trembled and held my face there for a few moments.

"Stay on your knees."

I stayed on my knees. She walked over to the wall; picked out a leash about six feet long and attached a collar…when the collar was buckled around my neck a small pad lock secured it. The leash was then hooked to the collar and secured to a ring on the wall.

"Get up… stand on your feet and take off the briefs… now… move."

I stood up and said nothing. I still had a buzz on from the Saki. As I removed the briefs I saw the open nipple bra drop to the floor. Tech stepped back just out of reach for my leash. I could clearly see those red glazed ridged nipples sticking out…then she stepped forward.

"Grab each of my tits with your hands and suck my nipples… hard," she said as she grabbed my head again.

She moved my head from one nipple to the other…over and over… then moved my head up to her lips and kissed me with a deep long sensuous kiss that ended by gently biting my lips.

"Lay down on your back."

I could only move so far with the leash. Tech wrapped what I later learned was a cock belt tightly around the base of my cock. The device was to keep you erect even after having an orgasm.

Tech stood on her high heel boots as she straddled me and bent down. I could feel the fishnet texture on my shaft as her hand shoved my throbbing rod into her wet twat. I grabbed her ass with both hands as she pumped up and down. I was so hot there was no way that I could hold it any longer...five thrusts... .I exploded. I let out a scream that I could n' t even hear. I was completely gone. The French call an orgasm "la petite mort" (the little death). At that moment I really knew what it meant.

"Oh my god...Oh my god!" Was all I could hear from Tech.

We were both spent. We showered separately and met in her master bedroom. The Asian motif was set off in black and white with Japanese screens. The king size bed was low and so was the lighting. Pungent Jasmine incense set a romantic mood.

Tech wore black thigh top nylons and black high heels with a strap around the ankles. She explained that those were bedroom shoes only, and the straps were there so they wouldn't come off when she has sex in bed. We engaged in pillow talk.

"Do you know why atheists can't enjoy sex...because they have no one to call on when they have an orgasm," she laughed.

Tech used humor to break the tension. She knew that I just had an outer space experience. She then looked into my eyes and became very serious.

"Paul, I want to tell you who I am and what I do. I'm a dominatrix; that's what I do as a business. Wealthy or powerful men in high places pay me a great deal of money to humiliate them, spank them, piss on them, flog them or whatever else they desire... when I told you on base that I was in charge... you can guess why. I have videos in a safe deposit box not only in New York but elsewhere as well... mostly of high ranking military officers, politicians, bureaucrats, and corporate execs."

"Do you feel safe...I mean you could be a target."

"Actually, I feel very safe because everyone knows if I die an unnatural death all the videos are released to the media."

"So you gave me a taste of what you do... like you said... to teach me...like a mentor."

"A very small taste baby... did you like it?"

"I don't believe I would be into that... but since it was you it was a turn on and it was really different...I never made it so hard in my life .. .It was really hot when you used words like cunt and tits.. .like you weren't holding back."

"I' m also bi-sexual...do you know what that means?"

"Uh... that means both men and women turn you on in sex?"

"Yeah, I mostly prefer women but I like situations... ah like situational sex... by that I mean like you...eighteen... smart... they have to be smart... I can't handle stupid... I never have sex with my clients... only bondage and discipline... I might make them jack off and punish them for it.. .I make them lick up their cum and swallow it... then I flog them... but I never have sex with them... our session was just to give you an idea of what it' s all about... in fact I'm a Capricorn and turned thirty six in January... but I've only had sex with three males... one in high school, one in college and now you.

"Tech that makes me feel really special... flattered...I feel honored... truly."

"And so you ought to," (she smiled seriously) "I've had sex with at least one woman for every year of my life... I have a girl friend I like who is coming here in a month... maybe you will get a chance to meet her and maybe even have a threesome...that means you me and her."

I thought to myself...oh god would I love that. Tech told me about her nipples. She went for acupuncture while in Thailand. She had one inverted nipple, but the female doctor told her she could bring it out. In fact it was a vacuum like cup that extended the nipple outward. She used them on both for a couple months until she liked what she saw: ridged nipples that stuck out further. They were hot, almost sticking out like thumbs. She discovered a red dye from a plant that among other uses give a reddish tint to the skin.

She recoats her nipples every six to nine months with the dye.

Pillow talk led to more sex. We fell asleep at around three A.M. The rest of the week end was a bacchanal of sex, food, dancing and of course going to our Jazz club the "Cock and Bull." Unfortunately, three weeks later everything changed. Tech was transferred to Germany. We had two more sessions but no weekends. The party was over and I never did get to meet her girlfriend. Tech wrote to me a several times, but we became as we are now, a memory to be marveled.

CHAPTER 13

———•———

WHEN I WALKED INTO THE Army National Guard Armory I could see that things had seriously changed. The evening drills had given way to week end drills.

"Hey VeHorn, welcome back... did they kick yer ass up there?" The lieutenant laughed.

"Every day and twice on Sunday sir."

"I understand that you start college in two weeks...in the meantime I want you to work full time here and help us catch up... at full time pay of course... from now on you are permanently assigned to me as my administrative assistant."

"Yes sir...it all sounds great."

"By the way, a Warrant officer you were assigned to gave you one hell of an outstanding report...4 A.. way to go... I'm submitting a recommendation for promotion effective immediately."

The situation was critical for all Army National Guard units in the segregated southern states. They were gearing up for a showdown against racial integration. Riot control training was number one on the agenda. Our battalion had six companies of approximately twelve hundred men located throughout counties on the West Coast of Florida. I'm detailing this because of what happened next. The companies were: headquarters (my unit), heavy weapons, armored infantry, mechanized infantry, combat support, and artillery.

My job was to go to each of the companies and certify that every man had received riot control training. A letter to that effect was to be signed by the C.O. and placed into each man's personnel file. Riot control maneuvers were to start at the first week end drill in January.

"Go home (N word), Go home (N word)."

We were ordered to scream this in unison as we practiced to clear the streets. Each formation would be headed by an armored vehicle followed by two squads of infantry. The orders were to have no ammo for our rifles only bayonets. However many of the guys had a revolver called a combat masterpiece hidden in shoulder holsters under their fatigues. This six round thirty eight caliber weapon was typically issued to Air Force flying crew to serve two purposes. One was for personal protection if shot down, and the other was to use in case the plane caught fire...a grim choice. Personal weapons were not allowed... that was largely ignored.

The lieutenant was a Korean War vet from Chicago and we were both Chicago Cubs fans. He was completing his degree work at the same college I attended. He had a dry sense of humor...we would know what he meant but it would go right over the heads of most guys in the company.

"Lieutenant, you know that go home (N word) is going to start a riot...why the hell are we yelling that...or is that the plan?"

"Hey VeHorn, this is the south and those are the orders... do it or get court martialed."

Even though we both agreed we were between a stone and a hard place, we had to follow orders. I felt like the WW II German Soldiers who said, "I vas only vollowing der orders!" Essentially, I was being ordered by the State of Florida to use the (N word).

Incredibly there were people at that time who actually believed that we were going to confront U.S. Army Airborne Troops... one of the toughest divisions in the Army. Some time before this The Federal government had sent Airborne troops to Little Rock Arkansas to integrate the schools. In retrospect I don't know what the hell these people were thinking.

Thank god we were never called up for riot control duty. That outrageous cluster fuck was the last straw. It was at that point I made my decision to get out of this chicken shit outfit. Since I enlisted before my eighteenth birthday, after three years I had the option to transfer to inactive status as a full time college student in good standing. That's exactly what I did.

My tour of duty was not over. I had one last two week active duty bivouac to "enjoy" with my battalion. We drive at forty five mph nearly four hundred miles by convoy in jeeps, three quarter ton trucks and two and a half ton trucks. The vehicles had no air conditioning, and of course it had to be during the last two weeks of July yeeeeha.

I was sort of lucky in a way, being assigned to a three quarter ton communications van. My job was to maintain radio contact with the lieutenant. His orders were to co-ordinate the convoy... no easy task. I had a driver...oh did I have a driver... his last name (changed of course) could have been Zeke or Clem. His name was almost that bad, since his first name was his mother's family surname and his last name of course was his father' s family name. For our purposes we will call him Clem. Now poor Clem had been on active duty for three years in Korea and in the Guard for over eight years. He was still a buck private because of his drinking. He had made it to the rank of corporal at least five times and to private first class more than that. He was a damn good mechanic though, and that' s why they kept him.

The ninety degree heat pierced through the canvas roof of the three quarter ton truck. My wet fatigues, stained with white streaks from my body salt clung like chamois. I dozed off in fits and starts interrupted by the van radio.

"STRAC five... STRAC five... this is HQ... over."

I picked up the receiver which by now as nearly as hot as an iron.

"This is STRAC five...over."

"VeHorn, we' re coming up to a junction in about three miles... bear to the right...MPs will be there directing the convoy...got that?" The lieutenant asked.

If we find a fork in the rode take it...over," I laughed. "Yeah too bad he doesn't play for the Cubs... over and out."

The last thing I saw were the MPs at the junction directing the convoy. With the drone of the truck motor and the heat I fell asleep. I would take a spell driving to give Clem a rest so taking a nap was authorized.

Bam...Bam...Bam... the truck was hammering through a corn field. I looked over and Clem was sound asleep... no, make that passed out with his foot on the accelerator. I tried to reach over and hit the brake with my boot but a vodka bottle was stuck under the brake pedal.

"What the fuck... son of a bitch...wake up Clem you asshole...you're drunk." I screamed.

There was no waking him. I turned the ignition switch off, but the truck kept rolling. I tried to reach over and pull the emergency brake but I couldn't get past. Clem was all sprawled over in the driver's seat. Then the damn radio came on...that's all I needed.

"STRAC five... STRAC five... come in...Where the fuck are you?"

It was the lieutenant. I finally ground the gears as I slipped the stick shift out of fifth gear into neutral. I had to sit on that idiot Clem's lap in order to press the clutch. The truck finally stopped rolling.

STRAC five...STRAC five to HQ...over."

"Goddammit VeHorn, where the hell are you...I got the MPs looking for you." The lieutenant was pissed off.

"Sir, we're out in a cornfield so I'm not sure where we are but I'll take a compass reading."

"Was Clem driving?"

"Yes sir."

That was pretty much the end of it. Clem got an article fifteen... that is two hours extra duty for two weeks. I got some private off one of the deuce and a halves (i.e. two and a half ton trucks) to be my driver. All the guys in the company thought this was funny, and joked abut it...until we went on maneuvers. That's when the fun really started.

During the second week of maneuvers we would have "war games" and face the aggressors. The aggressor force was made up of specially trained Army Airborne units. These troops had not only different uniforms, but they also had their own "language." All Army units would face them as the enemy in maneuvers. However, their favorites were The National Guard groups. Their job was to "kill" or capture as many personnel as they could. If you were captured you would be subject to very harsh POW treatment.

Your hope of course would be to have the field referees designate you as terminated. We never did defeat them. In fact it was set up that way. The whole idea was to see how well trained you were.

"I got my ass captured last year... those bastards were tough... they had me for two days... all we got to eat was bread and water... they tell you to be a traitor so things will be better... and no sleep." One of the drivers said.

"So the idea is to be a traitor and...no problem...right?" I said sarcastically.

"Yeah VeHorn, and they slap the shit out of smart asses... so you know what they'd do to you." He sneered.

A lot of the guys didn't like me, but they all respected me because I could put their dumbasses on duty reports. So for the most part it was like a Mexican standoff. They also had no way of getting a pass during active duty training except through my office.

The red dust was settling on grass and vines by the side of the road. Armored vehicles, and trucks, and infantry units all left their marks in the sand. Clouds of dust and clamor of tanks dissolved into the twilight. The scent of coffee here, and cigarette smoke there blended with the clean smell of gun oil as soldiers readied their weapons. Was tonight the night? Would the attack be here... on our flanks... where? The questions hung in the air while troopers, nervous as night neared crouched low in their fox holes. Sleep was not an option. The sound of crickets made the whole scene feel hollow as the sun was fading in the West.

Red and white and blue streaks reflected from a purple haze in the sky. Dusk was now the order of the day.

The lieutenant and I were in the headquarters bunker scanning the horizon with our field glasses. In case the enemy would send in a recon patrol, we needed to see it. The two lane road lay somewhat below us and stretched into the distance. Eight miles down that road would lead you to a paved road which would go to the main gate and straight into Savannah.

"VeHorn, do you see that jeep?" The lieutenant asked.

"Yes sir and I see who's in it."

Unless you had a pair of high quality binoculars with coated lenses it would be impossible to make out the occupants. We were the only ones that had that type in the bunker. The standard Army issue binoculars were primarily for field use. These were used for Navy and Air force as well as Army artillery units.

"Son of a bitch...that's the CO and the top kick (i.e. company top sergeant)...in class A uniforms... those assholes are going into Savannah to party...while we sit here in these fucking holes."

Nobody else could hear him since we were alone in the elevated observation area. A one foot strip between the sandbagged bunker gave us a view of the horizon.

"That should be us sir," I scoffed.

He was really put out about it, and he had a reputation for getting even. It looked as if an idea had come to him. We now knew for sure that the attack would not be tonight or they would not have left. Only the exec officers and the company COs knew of the night and time of the attack. Junior officers and non commissioned officers (sergeants etc.) did not know.

"VeHorn, get on the radio and get the engineer platoon's Warrant officer over here."

The Warrant officer was combat engineer vet from both Korea and WWII. The guy was tough and had a marine salvage business. We will call him Brandt (not his real name of course).

"Warrant officer Brandt, these aggressor guys are ruthless...so here' s what I want you to do..."the lieutenant went on.

The idea was as devious as it was creative. The plan was for the engineers to remove the two by fours and canvass over a fifty eight foot long slit trench latrine which was parallel to the side of the dirt road. He didn't want anyone to get hurt. He told them to put charges on the latrine side opposite the road so the latrine contents would blow up and out over the road.

"A shit storm.. .I love it... god dam em," Brandt laughed.

"At the first sign of em I'll give the order and you hit the plunger... got it?" The Lieutenant smirked.

The Georgia pines were spider web like as the waning half moon bathed them in silver. Whippoorwills called out and crickets chirped incessantly. The hills, the road, and even the camouflage had a sacred look in the cool southern night...as the lieutenant peered intensely through his binoculars at the shadowy road.

I remember the exact time, it was two fifty-six A.M.

"VeHorn, grab your binocs...you see black out light slits?"

Army jeeps had two black out lights each having a rectangular slit. The lights were just enough to see ahead about ten feet, but could still be seen from a distance by the enemy on a dark night. In a combat zone the lights were turned off, but gunners would fire at the sound regardless.

"Black out lights sir."

"VeHorn, radio engineers... contact... fire on my command."

I radioed the word " contact"...then..."ready to fire on my command." The lieutenant waited for just the right moment...which seemed forever...I had my earphones on and my binocs in my left hand with the radio mic in my right... their jeep was precisely at parallel center.

"Fire!" The order was loud and clear.

I relayed the "fire" order. The night exploded and the shit storm commenced in more ways than one. We could hear the CO and top kick swearing violently...at the same time we were laughing like mad.

Suddenly the whole battalion commenced firing. There was an orgasm of firing from weapons of every size and description. Dozens of parachute flares lit up the sky, one-o five mm. howitzers, mortars, tank cannons, machine guns, rifles, all firing hundreds of blank rounds. The fourth of July was two weeks earlier, but this was the best fireworks display I had ever seen. Nearly ten minutes passed with me just roaring with laughter. Then the field phone rang. It was General Petty.. .not his real name, but the word petty fits because he was petty... and for some reason he was angry. I had no idea why he should be so upset. He also sounded as if he had one drink too many. I thought " uh oh." It was so loud I could hardly hear him. I only saw the red light flash on the field phone when he called because I couldn't hear the ring tone.

"God dammit... god dammit... god dammit." Seemed to be all he could utter.

This was getting even better. I held my hand over the phone so the General couldn't hear me. I was in a state of convulsive laughter. At that point one of my buddies crawled up to the HQ bunker he was a super sharp med student. A silver flask filled with a top shelf scotch was handed to me. The timing was perfect. He knew it was a SNAFU (i.e. situation normal all fucked up) and was laughing like hell. The general continued to scream into the phone.

"Cease fire god dammit... cease fire... cease fire!"

I could almost hear him and I knew damn well and good what he was saying so I did the well worn radio trick.

"SSShhhhwaa... shiiiish... shwashwashwa... I can hardly hear you sir...it's too loud." After more shwashwa... the radio static sound I was making worked... he hung up."

The bombardment went on for another twenty minutes until someone finally started shooting red flares up as a signal to stop firing. I guess a lot of units didn't know what the red flares meant or they just were having too much fun. After nearly forty five minutes of continuous shelling the firing stopped.

This is the most incredulous part of all. The general's aid, a major, drove up in an army command car the following morning... what a show... a driver... the major's aid... and of course flags on the command car.

"Lieutenant, were you in command here at the HQ when the attack occurred?"

I couldn't believe what I was hearing. Attack... what attack...this was going in a whole new direction.

"Yes sir." The lieutenant said sheepishly.

I could tell by the look on the lieutenant's face what he was thinking. It was now going to be his turn to get hit by the shit storm. I thought that drumming him out of the Guard was the next step. I had visions of the French movie Beau Geste...only this time with the lieutenant standing at attention in front of the battalion while the general rips off his epaulets, and gold buttons... with the final coup de grace... the breaking of the lieutenant's saber over the general's knee... ah... but nay, nay monsieur ... not zo vast! Besides, the lieutenant didn't have a saber, so obviously that would never work.

"The general wants to congratulate you on the outstanding defensive firepower you delivered in the face of an attack by aggressor forces." The major said seriously.

The general had written this letter to be read to the lieutenant. In fact the letter became a part of the commendation the battalion received. Not only that, the lieutenant was promoted to captain, and he subsequently promoted me to sergeant. The CO and top kick couldn't say a word because technically they were AWOL. They just sort of had to eat shit so to speak.

We of course never did have to face the aggressor forces as such during that two week active duty session. That battle had been fought. When we returned home I was doing the accounting for our two weeks of active duty. I discovered that the cost of the ammunition was budgeted for only a one time charge. They had no choice, either double the cost for the ammo that was shot up or promote the rascals who were responsible.

You just can't make these things up... ask one of my favorite authors, Carl Hiaasen, a fellow Floridian. This is "Freaky Florida" after all. Just remember; follow the money.

CHAPTER 14

———◆———

FLAKES OF SNOW WERE DRIFTING over the parking area as I rushed to class.

A winter of wonder, since the West Coast of Florida rarely gets snow. My winter was doing just fine, hot in fact. This first semester was becoming a concert of romance, sex, politics, and freedom. Learning became more than memorizing. One of my great Psych professors was a student of Socrates.

"Know thyself," Dr. Goldberg (name change of course) admonished.

Those were the first words out of his mouth to every new class. Goldberg was brilliant. He graduated from Columbia with his Ph.D. in behavioral psychology at twenty two years old. He made sure that within the first five minutes of his lecture he would mention his membership in MENSA. He and I established quite a rapport. He made a distinction between God and religion, saying that religions made up the rules as they go along. We had in depth sessions lasting late into the evenings where he would expound on his theories.

"My God is better than your God is the mantra that goes on and on... you know there have been more atrocities committed in the name of religion than any other reason.. .I honestly don't get it... People who hate Jews pray to Jesus, a Jew... believe in the gospels written by Jews.. .St. Paul was of course a Jew and was the most prolific of writers of the New Testament... St. Peter was a Jew and he is the rock on which the church was built?"

Dr. "G" was right. It was one of his concepts that seared itself into my mind set forever. The irrationality of it all is overwhelming. We can ask why, but the answer is will never be found. The madness of man is inexplicable.

"You want to make a lot of money VeHorn?" He always called me VeHorn... then you need to start your own religion....in America that's easy...any low grade moron can start one... you just collect all the money and throw it in the air... all the cash god grabs he can keep... whatever hits the ground is yours... tax free!" He laughed sarcastically.

He was well known for his biting sarcasm; in fact he had developed it into an art form. He skewered many students who tried to dazzle him. One jock tried that and went down in flames right in front of mostly female nursing students in his psych class.

"Well Mr. Davis, if you can't dazzle them with brilliance then baffle them with bullshit... right? But one word of advice to you sir... never try to bullshit a bullshitter."

The class just roared... Dr. "G" had struck again. The jock's face turned crimson as he scooted down at his desk. He never returned to the class again. We found out that he had withdrawn from the psych class. Hopefully, he learned to not try to embarrass a professor.

" I understand that you have a way with the ladies VeHorn... of course you have an edge having had those sexual experiences... and already having been in the service... as a psych prof I frequently become the father confessor for female students...a number of them are infatuated with you."

I had told him all about the Lana and Tech experiences without mentioning names; never, never kiss and tell. He was both amused and interested as a psychologist. He would invariably go to the "why" level.

"Do you know why the ladies like you? Because you listen to them.... in fact, by the way they talk I surmised that you listen them into bed."

I was in shock and awe...I listen them into bed....Doc was not too far off the mark. In my mind I reviewed some of my "experiences." He was right. I didn't really know why things were going my way, but now I had a pretty good idea.

"That of course and your column in "The Omnibus" (our weekly college paper... not the real name)... nice name "For Men only" you know that's the first thing the women will read," he chuckled.

Every week the photo of a girl appeared in my column as "the cutie of the week"... which turned into a fierce competition among the co-eds. It was candy land for me. No proposition went unheeded. Of course any indication of impropriety was and will always be vehemently denied by "moi." All of the "cuties" wore bathing suits. Unfortunately, some of the guys wouldn't let their girl friends pose; they had absolutely no sense of humor.

Drive-in movie theatres were the place to go. They were called passion pits for obvious reasons. Many of them were so filled on Friday and Saturday nights that managers had to close the gates.

The popcorn caper, as I call it, became legendary on campus. Now I had heard about this "technique" before but I thought it was an urban legend…not any more. The largest department on campus was the nursing school. More women than men attended this college, which was not typical at that time.

"Hey Horney, I hear you've got a date with the ice queen for Saturday night," my friend Jay said with a grin.

"How did you hear about that already?"

"In the student union at lunch from the nurses… man not even you will get to first base with that one."

Everyone knew that I never talked about who I had made it with. That was my rule number one. I told the girls "no one will ever know"…so the word was out. VeHom doesn't kiss and tell.

"I just asked her at around ten this morning…I guess she couldn't wait to spread the good word."

" I' ll bet it won't be that easy to spread her legs… you know what they say, the ice queen won't melt." Jay was having way too much fun.

"You know me… no one will ever know."

I had acquired a used cream puff luxury Chrysler sedan from an estate sale. It turned out to be the perfect playboy playpen. My friends called it my pimp mobile; jealousy is so obvious. The plush, comfortable bench style power seats were seductive. I replaced the interior lights with red bulbs. The setting spoke for itself. My mother said the car had "come hither and wither" written all over it... she added that I better wear condoms and don't get anyone pregnant.

Birth control pills were a blessing and it seemed like every girl was on them. Unfortunately, abortions were legal only in New York State at that time. The tragedy of not having legal abortions else-where in the U.S. was that so many girls and women died from botched abortions. That's when we had a real separation of church and state without some putrid politicians dictating to women what they can and can't do with their bodies. It's very simple... if you don't believe in abortion don't have one... but keep your noses out of other people's business.

The excitement was swelling, among other things, as I knocked on Gail's front door. ".

"I'll be home by one." She called to her parents.

As we walked to the car the typical small talk ensued. Her blonde hair as usual was tightly woven in the back and twisted over her head. In spite of the cold her blouse was rather low cut.

We parked in our space at the drive-in. Gail's skirt was hiked up above her nylons so that the garter just showed. I put my arm around her and as she snuggled up to me and gave me a long deep tongue in mouth kiss. This could not be the ice queen guys talked about. Just as suddenly she moved back to passenger side of the car.

"Don't try that again or you can take me home," she said angrily.

"Hey, wait a minute, you came over here and kissed me."

"I don't want to discuss it or we can leave."

The air was thick enough to cut as we sat quietly watching the movie. Then she slid over again, this time putting her hand on my chest.

" I' m sorry; it's just that I'm just so shy"

I could feel her orbs pressing against me as she ran her tongue up my neck. I began to breathe heavily, obviously turned on. This time she again scooted to the other side of the car.

"You are being way too forward, and I don't like it."

I didn't know what kind of game she was playing, but there was a name for females like this. Gail was a prick teaser. She apparently got off on turning men on and then turning them down. She pulled this stunt a third and fourth time. On the fourth time she cried and said 'forgive me' but that too was a ruse.

There were always two movies at the drive in with an intermission in between. I went to the concession stand and got one box of popcorn and two small colas in a tray. The popcorn boxes had flaps on the bottom which were closed. The top flaps remained open. When I got to the car, I sat the tray with two colas on the roof, opened my fly and slipped my cock in through the bottom flaps. It was dark, so there was no way to see it. Then I held the popcorn box in my left hand with my right hand I tapped on the window. She opened the door and I passed in the cola tray. I scooted into the seat, got the door closed and we started having our repast of popcorn.

"Oh my god...you bastard... you nasty bastard... take me home... take me home now," she screamed.

I was laughing....I could hardly speak.

"Well, that sure beats what you find in a box of cracker jacks," I said through the laughter.

I had talked to Jay over the week end. When he asked how the date went I told him it was nothing special. I got to school Monday morning and ran into Jay on my way to the student union.

"You are so fucked... no, you are so unfucked." Jay said with tears rolling down his cheeks from laughing.

"What the hell is wrong with you?" I smiled knowingly.

"I had coffee with some nurses at the union... they told me about the cockorn." Jay was convulsing.

"Oh... that," was all I could say with a straight face.

"You won't be able to get laid at this campus with a hundred dollar bill."

At that point we walked back to the union to have coffee... then a funny thing happened. The nursing students were all looking at me. Most of them were smiling, and even laughing. Some of them of course were aghast; their problem not mine. One of the girls came over and invited us to sit with them at their table.

"You are so bad," they were saying as they laughed.

"Well, I'm not nice but I' m fun."

It was amazing. I expected to be ostracized by the entire female student body. I had more invitations for parties and dates after "The Great Popcorn Caper" than ever before. One of the sororities even had an election appointing me as their mascot. That involved attending all of their social functions, as well as being the escort for any girl who didn't have a date. Oddly enough, I soon found out that they were not having "dates" in rotation so that I would be with a different girl at each event...and what was Jay's reaction?

"VeHorn, you are one lucky son of a bitch."

And my response?..."ah yes Jay, but I am a first class son of a bitch, which means I am a son of a bitch with class."

CHAPTER 15

———————

POLITICAL DISCOURSE WAS BECOMING A hot item at that time, and conservative extremists were lifting their ugly heads. Just like now. The John Birch society as well as other neo conservative groups were infiltrating college campuses nationwide. An offshoot of these boneheads was the YAF or "Young Americans for Freedom." That freedom of course was limited for "WASPS" only (i.e. White Anglo Saxon Protestants). They operated almost like a fraternity, including a "rush" like fraternities have for members. Of course the membership was limited to men only. Does that have a familiar ring to it? Naturally I was "rushed" and made a member. I was over six foot, with blonde hair and blue eyes.

How could I miss? One couldn't help but notice the "Arian" overtones.

I told my political science prof that I had been "rushed" for this fine upstanding patriotic organization. By this time I had figured out what they really stood for. There was a lot of money behind them since they had retreats at a variety of exclusive country clubs and the like. Needless to say minorities need not apply. They had a pejorative term for every minority including Roman Catholic, Jewish, Hispanic, Asian, Black, and whoever else happened to be the minority de jour.

"VeHorn, the worst is yet to come... you haven't seen anything yet... power yields to money and money is behind this movement... you know what they say, money talks and democracy walks," was Professor Talino' s response.

Tony Talino had been at Anzio, Italy during the ill fated invasion there. His family came from Florence and he spoke fluent Italian. He was in Army intelligence as an interpreter. His combat experiences were rough, and he had been awarded the Purple Heart. Like my dad, he would never talk about what he had been through.

"More and more only kids whose parents don't have the money or the "juice" will wind up going to war... during the civil war the poor kids from the south had no choice while the rich kid's families either paid a poor kid to take their place or simply bought their sons out altogether."

Prof. Talino was really ahead of time on that one. We now know that during the Viet Nam war kids like George Bush and Cheney didn't go into combat. However, they sure were anxious to send other people's kids into their WMD trumped up Iraq war.

I left the YAF in short order. Not all the YAF member's families had the money or political pull to keep them out of the draft so they wound up in Viet Nam. I wonder if they ever learned anything.

Politics became ever more heated during the sixties. It's impossible to write this book with all of its "flavors" of my life and times without mentioning it. CNN did a special on the sixties, but it's just like seeing general video footage of a war.

In a war you can' t really see it until you smell the cordite from fired shells and hear the blood curdling screams of dying men from both sides crying out for their mothers. That's right, when men in combat are dying they scream for their mothers. I'll bet you didn't know that. I interviewed a number of veterans who were terminally ill. They knew that if they did not share their experiences they would be forgotten forever. They were mostly WWII vets but there were Korean and Viet vets as well. They told me these stories for the sake of posterity.

Many of these vets had permanent videos in their minds of the minutest of details.

"The freezing rain dripped from my helmet making a soup of the only hot meal we had in weeks as I sat in the mud of my foxhole... kernels of corn floated off of my cold tin mess kit half into the mud.. .I kept my eyes fixed on the picture of my girl.. .I sheltered it under my poncho...she was talking to me... machine guns were firing in the far distance."

"The Nazis fired their eighty eight mm. artillery rounds at the tree tops... hundreds of wood splinters pierced the bodies of the men... a man's arm hit my helmet... the blood oozed down my jacket...I tried to dig deeper into my fox hole...I heard screaming and screaming...It was me...I wasn't hit...I was just screaming."

"The worst thing was the stink... dead human bodies rotting in the jungle... dead animals... human waste…garbage...the heat made it worse...the Philippine Islands had hogs that would eat the bodies…I have nightmares about that."

These are a few excerpts of the interviews I had with so many vets. Many of them said they would not share these horrible memories with their families, but they would tell me...otherwise the pain of war would be forgotten forever.

The Nixon curse remains with us. That delusional little egomaniac is the only president in history that resigned in disgrace. His war on drugs did not include marijuana except as an afterthought. An acquaintance of mine from Miami was at Bebe Rebozo's compound when Nixon was there. He said they were talking strategy when suddenly a drunken "Tricky Dickey" Nixon said ' I hate them god dam hippies, put pot on that list too.' This meant his war on drugs list. That was the Nixon curse which essentially renewed the Volstead Act. It created a new group of gangsters growing and selling pot...generations of pot drug abusers who would get police records... billions of dollars worth of property confiscated by police and even more billions paid by the taxpayers to adjudicate and imprison people for using pot. In some states having half an ounce can result in up to five years in jail. What a brilliant idea... an idea whose stupidity surpasses only its ignorance.

Thank God I prefer martinis...shaken not stirred of course.

That's not all. Richard M. ' Your President Is Not A Crook' Nixon lied like hell in his method to end the Viet Nam War. He had a secret plan... so the gullible public voted for Richard M. (M for Moron) Nixon. His plan was secret alright...a month later he secretly invaded and bombed Cambodia without notifying Congress. Far more American casualties occurred under his time in office than before.

It has been said that America started going slowly down after the assassination of President John F. Kennedy... that the death of hope in America began with the death of JFK. I can only ask myself questions in that regard. Is America better off now than it was at the time of Kennedy? Is there less poverty? Is it possible to attend college without life consuming debt? Is there medical coverage for all? Is the society divided into the super rich and the rest?

Will America in the near future just be another Mexico? How long are we willing to spend blood and treasure to be the world's policeman? Is it liberty and justice for money? How long before another politicized Supreme Court appoints another president? Will the Supreme Court stop playing God by creating people out of corporations? Can we get an uncorrupt Supreme Court that won't equate free speech with money? Will we ever have a one man/one woman vote? Can we finally have separation of church and state? Will we ever stop gun killings? I don't have the answers... .as the song writer so aptly put it...the answer my friend is written on the wind.

A final item....I saw this on the internet...the writer is unknown but I will share it with you...or maybe you've seen it already....It's a parody...a sad parody of our pledge of allegiance.

"I pledge allegiance to the flag of the multinational corporations of America and to the republicans for which it stands, one nation under lobbyists with liberty and justice for money."

By the way, don't blame me...I'm only the messenger.

CHAPTER 16

———✦———

THE U.S. NAVAL BASE ON the Atlantic coast of this mid southern state was broiling under the mid July sun. I reported there for my two week's active duty.

"OC (Officer Candidate) VeHorn, reporting for duty." I said to the CIC (chief in charge) as I handed him my orders.

An OC at that time was in a way like a warrant officer. You are not an officer and you are not an enlisted person. You are called Mr. but not saluted and you are not called sir. The OC was under study to become an officer.

"Mr. VeHorn, report to the duty officer in building twenty six... at the Naval schools campus. You're assigned to UCMJ (Uniform Code of Military Justice) training for Navy and Marine boots (boots are basic trainees)."

All basic trainees in every branch of service are required to receive UCMJ training. In the event that they foul up there is no excuse. As in civilian life, being unaware of a law is not an acceptable reason for breaking it. The most common penalty is the "article fifteen" a rule that is a sort of catch all. Often times personnel will receive "article fifteen" for extra duty. That was the case because the NCO or officer didn't know anything else to charge him or her with. In other words, you did something we didn't like, and although there isn't a specific rule against it we will just give you an "article fifteen." It may sound unfair but it does serve a purpose. I know very few people who haven't received at least one during their career. They are not reported in your personnel file, so promotions aren't affected. I received one in high school ROTC for the white socks affair...which was highly unfair. Of course we all know that life is not fair. I received one in Army Airborne basic training because I was rightfully wearing a Private First Class Insignia when I arrived in uniform at the basic training center. No one said that you weren't to wear promotion insignia, so I guess the "article fifteen" seemed to fit the bill. The sergeant had me supervise a squad of guys who were doing lawn duty as my article fifteen penalty. I think that was more for effect, since you can't place a UCMJ charge without the person having had the UCMJ course. I never heard another word about it.

I have the utmost respect for the men and women cadre in our armed forces. Navy and Coast Guard Chiefs, Army, Air Force and Marine sergeants are the backbone of our military. Have you ever seen a group of recruits get off the bus or truck at a basic training reception center? There is no way that these people will ever make it... yet these drill instructors will shape them up in nine weeks to be sailors, marines, airmen, and soldiers. Miracles do happen.

"Your left... your left... hup... hup... to the rear march."

I was looking out of the office window watching my next class, a platoon (about forty four) of Navy and Marine boots doing close order drill on the "grinder." A grinder is a paved area where boots practice marching skills under the tutelage of a drill instructor ... sounds so refined doesn't it.

"Yer draggin ass third squad... platoon halt... right face...at arms length...drop down and give me twenty (push ups)." So it goes for refined.

This DI (drill instructor) was a marine "gunny sergeant." That is he is above a staff sergeant but below a master sergeant. I understand that the designation was artillery sergeant early on. These guys are amazing. Many of them are very sinewy, typically five six to five eight, have gravelly voices and look as if they just put on a new uniform. At that time they wore "smoky" hats like smoky the bear, and of course had a professional attitude. Oh, about that professional attitude...not like in civilian life... but as in..."for the next nine weeks I will make your life a living hell; do you understand?'

Two over head fans were whirring in the steaming classroom. The wind had shifted and now the open windows let in the stench of the local paper mills. I walked into the classroom.

"On yer feet!" The gunny ordered as all the boots stood at attention.

"Thank you gunny; take your seats."

The DI in these classrooms stood in the back of the room at parade rest during the presentation. Their sole purpose was to make sure no boot fell asleep. In fact I got the impression that they really wanted to catch one. This particular class was the last one of the day which ran from two to four PM with a ten minute break in between. These guys had four to five hours sleep the night before and had busted their asses all day.

I tried to keep it alive, as the fans droned on. Air conditioning was not an option. I saw this one marine boot nodding his head... then...bam...his head hit the desk. In that instant a shot streaked down the aisle...it was the gunny. Later, I heard a boot from New York say 'he took off like somebody lit his dick.' Actually, that pretty well described it.

"You were asleep boot...on your feet... on your feet," the gunny screamed while stomping both of his feet on the floor.

That was only the beginning. The marine boot suddenly stood at attention with the DI's face not eight inches from his own. There was a silence in the classroom like the still before a hurricane.

"Sir...sorry sir,"

Then the hurricane hit. We all were to discover that sorry is not a word a DI will use or hear. The gunny got even closer to the boot's face and yelled even louder.

"Boot do you know where sorry is in the dictionary?" His voice boomed.

"Sir...no sir."

"Between shit and syphilis," the gunny bellowed.

I had never heard 'sorry' described in quite that way before. Not even close. The guys in the class looked at me...we were all stunned. I was ready to laugh like hell; of course I knew that was a bad idea. I looked back at them as if to say, 'don't even think about laughing... don't even breathe.' The class resumed with the now wide awake boot standing at attention at the back of the class. Thankfully, the class ended.

"Class dismissed...platoon formation on the grinder." The sergeant ordered.

"Gunny, see me after class."

"What is it Mr. VeHorn?"

"Gunny if you're going to spring one like the 'sorry' let me know in advance... I never heard that before."

"You have now." He said as he did a sharp about face and double timed out the door.

You got to love these gritty guys. They aren't much for talk but they get the job done. I knew better than to challenge them. A lot of new second lieutenants and ensigns find that out the hard way.

A final comment about this combat decorated gunny...he always used the expression, 'I could care less.' One day I saw him after another class.

"Gunny, you know you always use the term, ' I could care less' ... actually when you say that there is still room for caring... If you say 'I couldn't care less ' then there is no more room to care."

At that point, the sergeant looked at me, blinked and never said a word. He did another sharp about face and double timed it out the door. From then on I never heard him say anything but, 'I couldn't care less. '

CHAPTER 17

———————

TEACHING IS PROBABLY THE FINEST thing I have ever done. You know what they say, 'those who can do, those who can do better, teach.' For my first year of teaching I chose an inner city high school in a northern state. The fact is that I may have learned as much or more than the students.

Since I had been a Navy Instructor it was decided that I would get several classes that were considered to have discipline issues. Lucky me, I thought. Someone had to do it and I thought I knew how to handle it. My method may have been a bit unorthodox, and by today's standards totally unacceptable...or not. I am a pragmatist... society's dictates can dictate elsewhere.

All of the students in my freshman class had juvenile delinquent records. That didn' t concern me. My job was to teach them English, not to judge them based on their past records. That, however, wasn't how the department head or members felt.

"Hard ass them VeHorn, that's the only thing they understand... besides this school would be better without their kind." The department head said in a mean tone.

Delusions of grandeur were a part of the department head's personality since his wife came from a prominent family in the area. Her obesity must have reduced her marriage prospects within her family's social network...thus resulting in his good fortune. The word was that they indeed had a fortune. There is an ancient German saying..."if you marry for money you will earn it." Kowtowing to wealthier family members can at best be demeaning...of course if that doesn't bother you then kiss away.

The first day of class with my "JDs" was a surprise.

"My name is Mr. VeHorn, I am your instructor and these are your records," I said as I pointed to the stack of files on my desk, "I have no interest in looking at them...you start here with a clean slate unless you choose otherwise...I couldn't care less what you have done in the past my only concern is what you are doing here and now...I am a Naval Instructor and teach Navy and Marine boots so there will be discipline in this classroom...you will be addressed as Mr. and Miss unless you want to be treated like children."

I was more than surprised...I was shocked. Not one sound was made when I announced that all students would be seated in alphabetical order. To this day I don't know if they were scared of me...which I doubt from this group...that I would look at their files or that they would be treated like children.

"Furthermore, don't make me look bad...I respect you and you will respect me...I will have this class be the number one freshman English class in its lane at the end of the year...you will all top the state exam for this grade."

By god, they did it. Of course the department head was out of sorts when the class did come in first. He held and inquiry to see if any shenanigans had taken place. Why is it that jerks always have to re-enforce the fact that they are indeed jerks? We were adjudged to be clean by a review staff from administration.

I had that class pretty much in hand from the start due to their "JD" records. The other classes were a different story. Some were smarter, some were not as smart, and some were meaner. Sophomores and juniors made up the balance of my classes. I used the same intro with each class as I had with the freshman class. The difference was that I had no files as such.

"Screeeeech!" the loud spine chilling sound of my finger nails on the chalk board got immediate attention.

"Oh don't do that again, eeeewu."

About ninety five percent of people really hate that noise. I am in the other five percent. After I had made my presentation I told the students to sit in alphabetical order. I was not thrilled to hear grumbling about my order.

" How dare you have the temerity to not follow my orders without whining...if you insist in demonstrating this bad behavior I will scrape the chalk board again...actually I love jazz and I rather enjoy the sound." Internally I am really enjoying this, while showing a serious face.

The classes all reacted the same way. They looked at each other in disbelief. The look on their faces said, ' where did this guy come from?' I would teach by walking around the room, often standing in the back of the room. Teenagers pay more attention when you are somewhat unpredictable with them. If a note were passed in class I would intercept it.

"Well Miss Jones (for example) I have in my hand a note which you have passed in class"...invariably a girl would break into tears..."Don't cry, I have no intention of reading this to the class or even to read it myself... unless of course you pass another note or get out of line in class in the future...in the meantime the note goes into my intelligence file at home where it will stay until such time it is ever needed."

Oddly enough the students really appreciated the fact that I left their dignity intact. Virtually all of the teachers would read an intercepted note aloud in class. I didn't feel that was fair. I would rather have the leverage of them knowing that if they pass another one or get out of line that they would pay the price by having the note read in class later. The worst part about that was that by then they may have a different girl or boyfriend.

Zounds...curses... not that...anything but that! I was more than happy to explain that fact to them when I intercepted a note. I would always have the caught student write a short paper about "The Sword of Damocles" and explain how that related to the note in my possession. Strangely enough they loved it, saying it was worse to have it hanging over their heads.

The first bit of lit that I would teach was Poe's "The Pit and The Pendulum." Of course that was the perfect story to get across the idea of holding any passed notes.

"What is wrong with you people...the dean wants to know why some of you cut other classes but come to mine...you must be devout masochists...this is the most highly disciplined class in this school...I would cut my class first!" I grinned as I said it.

"Because you're fair and more fun," they would all laugh.

"Balderdash...balderdash...I say...you will ruin my reputation." I said tongue in check.

We did have fun. They called me Monty Hall the host of "Let's Make a Deal" because I would willingly make a deal with them if they screwed up a test or missed a homework assignment. If they had a really creative reason I would make a better deal but not so much if it wasn't. Either way they would get a deal. Usually it was tougher than if they had done the job in the first place, but the students were elated with it.

One group was an advanced English class for juniors. I would always offer an extra credit question which hopefully was hilarious. We had finished a segment of Shakespearean sonnets and plays. I finally located an extra credit question for the exam...in which of Shakespeare's plays was there a dog?

"I deeply regret that not one of you very brilliant students failed to get the extra credit question right...and I had such confidence in you...it shakes the very foundations of my being to think that not one of my gifted students would miss the answer to such a profoundly simple question." I laid it on thick as I smirked.

"Why Macbeth of course... you remember when Lady Macbeth said... out out damn spot."

"Oh no Mr. V (all the classes were calling me Mr. V by now) boo... hiss... not fair." We were all laughing.

I would bet that they told that one to their kids... if you ever have a smart ass teacher who asks you in what Shakespeare play there was a dog etc. etc.

This was an inner city school and we did have our share of toughs. Some of these people would disrupt classes, bully other students and just be over all ignorant rectal orifices.

"So I understand that you can whip anybody in school."

"Thas right," Charles replied rubbing his right fist with his left.

"I am told that you have a team too, right?"

"I gotsa gang," Charles corrected me.

"Ah...let's call them a team Charles... kind of like the "A" Team, OK?"

"That be cool... whas up?"

"You have never passed English...how would you like to pass in my class?"

He was one of our "social promotion" students. As long as he attended class and stayed out of trouble he would receive a certificate of completion at graduation. This had a certain value since a future employer would hire him based on attendance and attitude.

"Whas I gotta do?" He asked curiously.

"Ok, here's the deal...number one you have to hand in a paper to me once a week on a subject we discuss in class because I have to prove I gave you at least a "D" grade for good reason... you have only gotten "Fs" or "S" for satisfactory completion in the past."

"What else I gotta do?" Charles wasn't too bright but he was no fool.

"In the first place keep your mouth shut about our deal...in the second place all I want you to do is to let people know that you like Mr. V and you will have a chat with anyone who disrupts his classes...do you understand?"

"Yeah I gets it... dat all I gotta do?"

"That's it one more thing I want you to start trying to use better grammar like...is that all.. .not dat... and that's cool not that be cool...I think that would make your mother happy.. .I'll help you with that."

Charles seemed really grateful. I could tell during the next couple of weeks that the would be problem students were very docile in my classes. I knew why...one day Charles asked if there was anyone I wanted him to chat with.. .he liked that word.

"No, you're doing a great job... no problems with any of the kids who give a hard time to other teachers...just keep handing in one paper a week..I noticed the papers are improving."

Without our deal Charles would not have lifted a pencil, so it really did help him.

"I wants to be in the Navy like you is...I mean...I want to be in the Navy like you," Charles was trying.

"That's a good goal to have...there are a lot of skills you can learn... your dad is a steel worker, maybe you can learn to be a welder for example," then he surprised me.

"I already a good welder, my brother has a body shop he teached me." Charles said proudly.

I didn't correct him that time; I acknowledged the fact that he had a skill. At fifteen years old, he was big for his age, about six foot and he lifted weights. Charles did fifty pushups without breaking a sweat.

Billy was what we would call a geek today... a fifteen year old with black rimmed glasses, slight of build and not as tall as his peers. Journalists were his heroes, and he made it clear to me that English was his most important class. Billy was in my advanced junior English class. Unfortunately he was the perfect target for bullies. His parents were divorced and he lived with his mother and sister. God knows where his father was so the family had a pretty tough time. I gave him a reference to the local paper where he became a part time copy boy.

"What happened to you?" I asked.

A black eye was still swelling, and blood from his nose was dripping on his shirt. He didn't say a word, but he laid his head on his arms at his desk. I sent him to the school nurse. He knew better than to tell on the bullies that beat him. Charles was in my last class of the day.

"Charles, see me after class...just want to go over the paper you turned in OK?" He came up to the desk after class, "Mr. V you wanna see me?"

"I want you to look into a matter for me... I have a student named Billy...who got his ass kicked by a couple bullies."

"I know who they be...I mean are."

"You know who beat him up...not some of your team."

"No sir... they be...I mean are... a couple mean white boys...they be... are...taken money from kids or they beat em up."

"I would like you to have a chat with them tomorrow...I guess they nailed Billy in the boy's restroom...remember you say nothing about our deal...oh yeah Billy makes straight "A's" in English maybe he can give you a hand with your papers."

"Mr. VeHorn report to the dean's office," came the message over the P.A. system.

As I opened the door to the dean's office there were four boys sitting on two benches. All of them had been in a fight. The two bullies looked as if somebody had mopped the floor with them. Billy's nose was bleeding again. Charles had no cuts or scrapes on his face but his knuckles seemed banged up. I couldn't tell if the blood on them was from his knuckles or the faces of the other boys. Charles kept his word and said nothing...thank god.

"Mr. VeHorn both Charles and Billy are students of yours...will you vouch for them? You want to give me a hand here...I'm trying to straighten this out."

Jack, the dean and I were being very professional in front of the boys. He knew damn well and good what went down... these two bullies were notorious.

"These two boys are saying that Charles here jumped them in the boy's restroom."

"Well dean those two boys are fairly good size and I wouldn't think one guy would jump two of them...looks to me like they tried to jump him then Billy stepped in to help his friend Charles and those two got the worst of it...looks like self defense to me... looks like those two are the culprits and ought to get punishment...you're the best judge of that."

One of the bullies cried out, "He's a liar Charles jumped us!"

"Stand up...you just called one of our faculty members a liar...that just earned you three whacks...bend over the desk," the dean said as he grabbed the paddle.

Poetic justice... the name caller got three whacks right on the spot...he even howled on the last two. The second one got the same treatment... he howled on all three whacks... the dean called him a co-conspirator.

"I' m not going to give you detention... but if I ever catch you two jumping a kid again I'll have your parents in here...alright all of you go back to class."

Jack started to laugh after they left. He was really a good guy. He had been in Nam early on serving his twelve months of Army duty in Saigon. He worked with the intelligence unit but still did a couple of stints in the bush.

"You are so full of shit...I love it...I've been after those two jokers since the beginning of school... that story about them jumping Charles almost made me laugh out loud... man, he really did a number on them...I figure they were working over Billy and you dropped a dime on them."

' Moi?"

"Yeah...moi...let's get a beer after work... meet you at the usual place about five... after that show I'm buying," Jack laughed.

Back to school night happened about two weeks after the bully boy incident. That is an evening when parents come to school to meet the teachers. I had a lot of my student's parents come to my classroom. Each session of the day was twenty minutes so that the parents could get an idea what the teacher was like. I think I was a curiosity because the kids would go home and talk about Mr. V.

Then the last period of the day came. This giant of a man walked in. He had to be six foot four at least and about two hundred ninety pounds. His arms between his elbow and shoulders looked like hams. He wasn't smiling. His wife was a large sweet lady with a big smile and a pretty hat. I just knew this had to be Charles' parents. I took a quick look at the window...we were on the first floor but it was still too high...I knew I wouldn't bounce. I hoped his dad was not unhappy with me.

A big broad grin spread across the dad' s face "you must be Mr. VeHorn... you be doin a good job with my boy."

Whew I thought what a relief. I had new respect for Charles...not only did he keep his mouth shut he had said good things.

The wife chimed in, "yes Sir Charles said you told him he is going to pass English this time."

"Yes ma' am, as long as he turns in a paper every week and he hasn't missed one yet...I think Charles is going to turn out to be Ok," she just beamed as I said that.

The following Monday morning Charles came to my classroom carrying a sweet potato pie his mom had baked for me. That was the lock; Charles got his "D."

After one more year of teaching in West Florida, and one year teaching college, I left the profession. I was a damned good teacher, and I really enjoyed it. Sadly, money was a factor. One year after I left teaching I paid more money in income taxes than I earned as a teacher.

Society gets what it pays for. A strong educated middle class results in a strong thriving democracy. Our current Supreme Court has politically appointed right wing judges who are undermining the very foundations of the middle class. By establishing that money is free speech under the first amendment simply means that those without money have no free speech. What a stinking pile of "Torro Fecundi." We now have state governors who are nothing more than pimps for a few greed driven, super rich, and would be oligarchs. Conservative state governors are establishing "right to work" states...a euphemism for "right to slave" states...they have banned teacher, police and firefighter unions. It will never change. The fate of America is sealed. The days of wine and roses of a thriving middle class with excellent schools and a happy society are over.

When I was a kid we believed in truth, justice, and the American way. Tragically the new American way is: lie, cheat and steal as well as, do unto others before they do unto you only do it first. One day the ninety nine per centers were demonstrating on Wall Street.

Above them, standing at a balcony of a large investment firm was a group of stock brokers and traders drinking Champaign and laughing at them. It reminded me of the famous Marie Antoinette statement, ' let them eat cake.'

Recently I spent some time in Silicon Valley with a friend of mine who had just sold his small software company to a giant firm. I don't know how prophetic he is, but what he said really floored me.

"You know VeHorn, there will be another American revolution but it won't be with guns and weapons as some think...that is way obsolete...it will be with cyber attacks."

He explained that economic inequality will be the cause. Corporate interests of the super rich will be brought to their knees through cyber attacks. The only choice they will have is to even the playing field or go bankrupt. He added that it has already started.

Life goes on.

CHAPTER 18

———————•———————

KACHUNK... KACHUNK... KACHUNK THE NOISE was deafening to the telephone caller on the other end of the line. Ralph was slamming his
desk drawer back and forth while he held the phone next to the
racket.

"It' s too late to cancel your quarter page ad...do you hear that...
the presses are rolling."

That was my first experience on my first day at the office of my new
sales unit. Each unit had their own separate six man office. My
training lasted for one month and it was intense. This was a directory company that did advertising throughout the country...with a
main office on Florida's West Coast.

These were the best and most well trained sales people I had ever
met. Selling became so fascinating to me that it was almost an
obsession. I read and still read about sales techniques. I watched
television evangelists; they are really superb salesmen. I would
watch them with the sound off to study their body language. One
of my speech Profs showed videos of Adolf Hitler without sound
to study his body language. It was frightening to witness. The Prof
called our attention to his co-ordination and eye movements. The

motions were almost hypnotic. Other examples of dictators were similar which means they were well rehearsed.

The unit sales manager was a piece of work. We had the number one unit in the country so he was careful not to piss anyone off too much. But Theodore had a real talent for pissing people off... that's not his real name of course but it makes the point as to what his real name happened to be. He liked to be called Ted, not Theodore. His nickname was Butch which he liked until someone told him what it could also mean. So of course we called him Theodore and sometimes Butch just to rattle his cage.

Ted was about five foot four and wore lift shoes. He said he was five foot six but we all knew better. His hair was perfectly styled and piled as high as possible every morning When we were on the road he would frequently have a wash and a set. GQ would have selected him as a model since Ted's clothes were always in fashion and sharp.

"You' re all fired... I am getting the paper work right now... you assholes!" Ted screamed as he sat down and his nose hit the desk.

Our team loved to play little games on him. On that Monday morning we screwed his office chair right down to the bottom. All five of us were laughing hysterically as he went out to get the termination papers. He had us all sign them, but he had thought better about firing us on the spot. He would lose way too much money and he would cost the general manager his bonus as well.

"I' m going to give you guys a break this time...I plan to keep these termination papers in my lock up...any other distraction and I will turn them in." His face was as stern as he could manage.

Of course we all had to sign them. We acted as if we were really concerned and seemed upset. So we signed them, there was Alfred E Neumann, D. MacArthur, M. Mouse, A. Lincoln, and of course G. Washington. Ted put them all into a large manila envelope without looking at the signatures and placed them into his locked filing cabinet. We had a key made for that some time before. Later that day we opened the filing cabinet, removed the termination papers and replaced them with gay porn magazines.

Late that afternoon we were all back in our office. Our "ring leader," not me for a change, spoke for the group.

"Listen Ted, we are all really sorry for that trick this morning and we would seriously appreciate it if you would destroy those termination papers...besides, we signed bogus names on them." Oscar pleaded as he hid a camera behind his back.

"You better have not put bogus names on them." Ted ranted angrily as he unlocked the drawer and jerked the manila envelope out.

Ted opened the large envelope and pulled out the gay porn magazines. At that moment Oscar started snapping pictures. Ted was startled at first from the flash and didn't really see what the magazines were. When he finally realized what happened he went after Oscar who was on his way out the door, running to his car, laughing all the way. Of course Ted never caught him.

Oscar had gotten four good photos and had them blown up to eight by ten sizes. They were masterpieces. When Ted came into the office on Friday morning the pictures were posted all over the offices and in the coffee shop.

"Wheew whew" ... people whistled...and..."Teddy Baby we didn't know."

"Why didn't you tell me Teddy?" One of the openly gay guys said to Ted.

After five on that Friday evening everyone in the office had to come in and turn in their paper work for the week. We really didn't get off work until about six thirty on Fridays. Then were all shocked. In walked Ted...in drag.

"Hi you thilly boys," he smiled speaking in a gay type voice.

His purse was pink with pink matching shoes. His legs were obviously shaved since you could see through his smoke colored panty hose. His very chic dress was a blend of maroons and it looked expensive. The wig was an auburn color. It looked as if he spent the entire afternoon getting ready. That was a very smart move on his part and the guys really respected him for it.

"OK big guy we'll take you out for drinks...in drag"..."Yeah in drag"... "you're cool man." The guys throughout the office were clapping and patting him on the back.

"Hey Ted that was about the smartest thing you could do...that took balls." I said to him as I spoke to him on the side.

"You ought to know Horny you're the psychologist...how was the effect?"

"Teddy baby, your stock definitely went up...I doubt if there is a guy in this place who would have the guts to do that...you da man."

Ted got drunk out of his gourd that night; as the designated driver I took him home to his wife. His kids were in bed. She was in on it.

"How did it go VeHorn?" She asked.

"I think everyone has a new found respect for Teddy after that act... no one could top that." I laughed.

Ted and I became good friends after that event. Of course that didn' t mean that I wouldn't stop the game playing. It would have been immoral to not take full advantage of Ted because...well...he was Ted.

Soon after I started with the new job I rented a really cool apartment at an upscale complex near the office. The decor said playboy all over it. The carpet was deep grey with a four by six soft white fluffy rug lying on top of it...I had to replace the rug a number of times. The living room furniture was black with chrome arms and rather stiff...which of course meant that the rug was the seating of choice. Large maroon pillows were propped against the otherwise uncomfortable couch with a glass top and chrome coffee table sitting by the side...a wine decanter and glasses on top of it. Jasmine scented candles were placed on the table as well. As I walked into the apartment the light switch turned on red lights and the stereo would begin to play late night jazz.

I hadn' t really planned it this way, but Ted took one look... all he could see was his fantasies come true.

"Oh my god...oh my god"...was all he could utter... "You give me a key to your place and I'll keep it stocked with booze and make you a key account rep...that means big bucks to you."

How could I refuse? He had to let me know when he wanted to use it and make sure I wasn't there at the time. There were a few over-laps, so two bedrooms came in handy. This was a ' win/win' and no one ever knew. I did a great job, but this was absolute job security.

Ted fancied himself as a latter day Romeo, especially now that he had easy access to a cool ' pad.' He would hit on everywoman he possibly could.

"It' s a numbers game VeHorn, for every one that says no, I'm that much closer to a yes."

"Yeah, I see that, on the other hand you have never gone to bed with an ugly woman but you have awakened with a few I've noticed... especially when we' re on the road." I scoffed.

"Fuck you VeHorn, and the horse you rode in on...I' m going to catch up with you," he grinned.

The following week we were sent to work a directory in the middle of the state. The incredible incident that occurred there is not only documented but is revealed to others only after an appropriate amount of drinking has ensued. This legend even has a title.

"The Night of the Tight White Shorts" it became known as. The upscale hotel where we were to stay for the next six weeks, except for weekends, had a high quality bar. All of the walls were mirrored and a background sound of low cocktail music set a sensual scene·. There was only one cocktail waitress and the bartender... a blonde bartender with big ' TaTas" (check your Spanish dictionary)...wear-ing a low, low cut white button up... actually buttoned open shirt... with a half bra that just showed a slight peek-a-boo pink of her areolas... and very, very, white tight, tight shorts. Her long white high heeled boots reached up to her knees. She was definitely not hired for her mental acuity.

It was a Wednesday evening around five thirty when the team returned from making calls. We all walked into the bar together except for Ted. Where was Ted?

"Oh I'm in love with her, the perfect woman...I yearn for her, and she is all I can think about...I would get divorced for her." Ted said wistfully.

That was the night before while we were sitting in the bar having a drink. Ted would look at her every now and then... they would smile at each other. He looked absolutely smitten...and he looked absolutely like an ass. He said he was going to stay over every week end just to be with her. He said he would tell his wife that he was going to play in a golf tournament...golf tournament?...sand trap Ted?

"Get a hold of yourself man... in the first place even your wife wouldn't believe you were in a golf tournament...divorce your wife? She will sue you for everything you have including your balls...and I don't mean your golf balls pal," I smirked.

Oh where, oh where was Ted? Why he was sitting at the bar way before we were supposed to be in-looking starry eyed at his beloved. I came in just a few minutes after the other guys got there. They were already having a drink and discussing the finer points of the blonde' s anatomy.

"I feel sorry for Ted, he really has an emotional attachment to this bimbo...unfortunately he's thinking with his wrong head," I declared.

"Feel sorry for him, are you crazy VeHorn? His ass is going get hung out to dry if he tries to divorce his wife." Derisive laughter came with the comments.

"Hey guys I'll be right back." I said getting up from the table where we all sitting near the bar.

I telephoned the bar from the outside pay phone. Tight whites answered.

"Hi, this is William Hunt...there has been a terrible emergency and my brother Mike has got to go to the hospital right now, would you please page him at the bar? His last name is Hunt."

"Ok, I'll do it right now." She said with urgency.

"Thank you so very much, may god bless you." I said that without laughing.

I quickly got back into the bar just in time to hear the page from Tighty Whitey Shorts.

"Mike Hunt! Mike Hunt! An emergency for Mike Hunt! Is Mike Hunt here?"

Everyone in the bar was snickering. I held my breath and kept from laughing out loud until she picked up the phone and said..."I'm sorry Mike Hunt isn't here."

I lost it. .. we all lost it and were laughing like hell.. .the tears were running down my cheeks... Tighty Whitey didn't get it...she missed it completely... The only thing the bar patrons could hear was my cunt and then my cunt isn't here... there was no distinction between Mike Hunt and my cunt.

At that point all I could see was Ted charging across the room from the bar screaming, "VeHorn you son of a bitch"

"Why me... why is it always me...I'm the victim here," and I lost it again.

Later that evening he took her to dinner and she spent the night with him. The next morning he was really hung over. I had breakfast with him.

"You were right, she really is dumber than a box of rocks...and I can' t believe she was such a bum fuck... she's really lousy in bed... we only had sex once and no BJ." Ted said sadly.

He never said he paid her but that question remains to this day. Of course he never considered the possibility that he was the bum fuck and he was lousy in bed. The male ego won't allow that no matter what the man looks like.

"Hey, Horney, look at this," Vito said flipping a business card off the wall.

The well known Cuban restaurant was a Florida West Coast business luncheon oasis. We actually had to stand in line to get in on any weekday. Dozens of business cards were posted on the huge cork board inside the entrance.

"A couple international airline business cards...these could be our ticket to candy land baby."

Vito was from Philly, and he had all the angles figured out. This one was going to be a masterpiece...with emphasis on piece... as in female.

"So what's your angle this time," I smirked.

"Horney, Horney, Horney, you have no artistic vision... see how lucky you are to have a Sicilian comrade... I have it all checked out." Vito was really excited.

Somehow, Vito and I got to be good friends if for no other reason than that we were both single and played the field. We were both carving notches in our respective bed posts.

From swinger parties to single bars we were in the scene. He was a top salesperson, albeit a little rough around the edges.

"Stewardess Administration...that's the ticket no, better than that... I'll be first vice president of stewardess administration and you'll be second vice president...I'll get the cards printed tomorrow."

At that time they were called stewardesses, but now they are call flight attendants. Just trying to clarify here and not being politically incorrect. God knows I've done enough of that in this book so far, and I really give a damn.

"Actually not a bad idea this time...so we'll use other names on the cards and we'll interview women for jobs...with strings attached of course." I said shaking my head.

" Bingo, you got it...we'll use them when we're out of town, say in some hick area...you know, where they're not that bright...

we're going to the north part of the state in two weeks," he laughed.

"You are unbelievable, but you're right... that scam would never work in Miami," I scoffed.

In two days Vito had perfect copies of the cards made complete with titles and names. We had two hundred fifty cards each.

"Hey, you think we have enough cards?" I laughed.

"Hey paisan we'll need a lot more!"

"So you call me paisan, my name on the card is Juan and I have blonde hair and blue eyes...oh that'll work."

"Yeah, I just say you work for our U.S. subsidiary...no sweat...so here's the deal."

Vito had it all worked out. We would approach women in clubs and tell them we are interviewing for stewardesses but there were a limited number of openings. Naturally they would improve their chances if they would like to play around. They would have to interview with one of us and then the other. Vito even had applications made.

Two weeks later we were at an average national chain motel in the northern part of the state.

Breakfast included a side of grits with the eggs and ham plus red eye gravy. I found the eggs and biscuits to be palatable. I left the ham, grits and red eye gravy on the plate. Vito sat down at the table he had red eyes but not from the gravy.

"You better put some band aids over your eyes before you bleed to death." I observed with a big smile. "Did you score?"

"Oh baby you wouldn't believe it...I never even told her she had to play around... she was all over me like a loose suit...you have an appointment with her tonight."

"So I get slippery seconds right? What did she look like? I know you Vito you probably had your beer goggles on."

"Come on Horney, she was okay, a little chunky but a great lay."

"Vito, do you know the difference between a dog and a fox? Six drinks...Hey, paisan, I know, you've never gone to bed with an ugly woman but you sure have been seen with a few," I laughed.

I passed on that applicant, but I was making out like a bandit without being "Juan." Vito would send his "interviewees "to my room anyway just to prove his scam was working. He was right; they just would come in and start to play. One of his better looking "job seekers" had sandy color hair and brown eyes. She started taking off her clothes as soon as I closed the door.

"Hi, my name is Sally, Fernando said that you make the final decision, but he said to tell you that I was so nice to him he knows you'll okay me."

Did I ever okay her. She had on an orange sun dress and white heels. Her bra and panties I was later to learn were in her purse because she had just left Vito's room.

"Sit on the bed Juan," She smiled.

With that she popped her thirty six rack out and pushed both of her nipples into my mouth. Naturally I couldn't say a word. The dress was suddenly on the floor and she was on her knees deftly unbuckling my belt and unzipping my fly. In an instant she had her hand around my cock. There was something not right about this.

"Wait a minute, why are you in such a hurry?"

"Well I'm late and my boyfriend will be out looking for me." She said trying to slip her mouth over the head.

"Stop...stop now!"

I jumped up, my interest in sex suddenly and abruptly over. In this little speed trap town,

I thought, it wouldn't take long for her country boy to find his heifer.

"Get dressed you have to leave right now, hurry up."

"Why?" She pouted.

"Just do it," I demanded.

She wasn't too happy, but she left. I packed my things on the run and called Vito. "Vito pack your stuff, we got to get the hell out of here... check out now."

"What the hell?"

"Don't ask...bad boyfriend."

With that I heard the phone hang up. I got to the motel lobby before he did. As I was checking out Vito came in to do the same. I was out the door.

"Follow me," I yelled.

I found out later that Vito had given twenty bucks to the motel manager to keep his mouth shut. His bribe probably saved us from getting our asses soundly kicked.

Sally had not seen my company car, but she did see Vito's car. He followed me over to a nearby supermarket and parked behind the store.

"What happened, did you get scared?" Vito sounded angry.

"Listen you schmuck, I'm not scared, I'm smart... she said she was late and her boyfriend would be looking for her...in this bum fuck burg he'll find her and us in a New York second."

Vito finally got it. I drove with him in my car back to the motel. We parked behind a line of trees and bushes. My car was hidden, but we still had a good view of the motel parking lot and property.

"What are we doing back here man; we need to get out of here." Vito said uneasily.

"Let's just wait here for a while... "I stopped in mid sentence.

It was about eight thirty, when a large pickup truck drove right up to the door of what was Vito's motel room. The truck's bronze colored paint reflected in the lights of the parking lot. A big guy, about six foot two and two hundred thirty pounds got out of the driver's side. He seemed to stomp around to the passenger side and yanked the door open.

He dragged a woman out of the truck by the upper arm and banged on Vito's former door. Although I had my window down, we couldn't exactly hear, but he was cursing and Sally was whining. During the whole time he kept pounding on the door.

"Damn Horney, we're lucky we got out of there." Vito said sheepishly.

He knew he had pushed the envelope too far this time. At that moment another big pickup truck arrived. A big hayseed, I figure over six foot and about three hundred pounds got out. He yelled something to the other cracker. Sally's boyfriend all but threw her back into the passenger seat and slammed the door. Both driver's got into their trucks and went to the office. They didn't stay there very long and left in a hurry. Right after that the cops rolled up.

"We've got to get a motel in another town...get this directory finished and get out of Dodge." I told Vito.

By this time we were both laughing like mad men, happy to be in one piece. By the following week we finished that directory and went back to our home base.

Vito being Vito couldn't give up that easily. He actually "sold" the idea plus the business cards to a couple insurance agents. He said he charged them two hundred fifty dollars each. I never saw a dime of that but he did buy a case of imported Cabernet Sauvignon for me.

Oh Yeah, there was one more thing. He told the insurance agents that there was a town in the northern part of the state where the scam worked perfectly.

CHAPTER 19

———◆———

HER WIDE BRIMMED BLACK STRAW hat made the blonde hair flowing down to her shoulders look all the more sensuous. She had a smooth black dress which showed an ample amount of cleavage. Designer snake skin shoes with a large matching purse almost said it all. The rest of the statement was made with a single Tiffany diamond hanging from a gold chain around her neck. She was obviously enjoying her mid thirties in elegance.

"Right this way Mr. Kingston." The currency broker said as he invited the couple into his office.

After leaving the directory company I acquired a series seven stock brokerage license, an insurance broker's license and a real estate license. An attorney I knew said he had a special situation that might interest me. He invited me for lunch at a local country club.

"VeHorn, as you know the stock brokerage business has gone wild...in fact fraud is rampant... my firm represents a securities house that needs an undercover broker." He kept his voice low.

"So Phillip, you thought of me...why?"

"We both know that you've done some clandestine work in the past and you can keep your mouth shut. You won't be the only one; we have people operating in several offices throughout the country."

So here I was in my own glass lined corner office at a prestigious stock brokerage firm. I continued glancing at this very attractive lady being escorted to the office next to mine. That was really the first time I noticed her Mr. Kingston.

"My name is Kingston and my lady here is Sylvia," He said with a British accent.

"Have a seat here ma'am." The currency broker said as he pulled up a chair.

As Sylvia crossed her legs I noticed an eighteen carat gold ankle bracelet on her right ankle. A slight smile played across her lips as she glanced at me out of the corner of her eye.

"I am here sir to do some currency trading today, so open your screen and let me see what's going on," he requested.

A tall slender sixtyish Mr. Kingston was doing his best to impress his lady. I could only presume that she was his mistress. He had no wedding ring on but she had a very expensive, elegant engagement ring.

"Mr. Kingston your losses are now over ten thousand." I heard the currency broker whisper.

This currency broker was a real Mr. Milquetoast. In fact he was truly a Mr. Wimpy Wimp. He was however married to a hot

Momma whose excesses included but were not limited to alcohol and affairs. Stay tuned more on that later.

"Please sir, I am perfectly aware of my standings, now buy the yen and sell the pound sterling." Kingston replied.

After nearly a loss forty thousand U.S. dollars later Mr. Kingston and his "mistress" left for dinner. The end of trading bell rang and all the brokers crowded around Mr. Milquetoast laughing and cheering him on. These guys showed no mercy.

"You sure stuck it to him, how much did you get him for," the comments continued.

I was once told that stock brokers were really ax murders in three piece suits. Many lawyers and CPAs became stock brokers strictly for the money of course. The entire scene of the mistress and the money reminded me of what my first Psych Prof said... 'The whole world revolves around money and sex.'

The regional vice president had to be told of course why I was there and to keep his mouth shut. He hated my guts and let me know it. The feeling was mutual. Unfortunately for him he knew what was going on and he was making a lot of money on brokers who had gone over the line. Ultimately he got his in more ways than one.

"The Holiday party this year will be held at the Horizon Club." The VP announced.

The low cut red and silver holiday dress my date, Gloria, wore was perfect. It was a black tie affair where we were welcomed at the door with Champagne.

"Oh my god who is that...I can't believe it." Gloria whispered

Gloria was a director of marketing; she was both funny and a good sport. Nothing shocked her much but this was an exception. Do you remember Mr. Milquetoast? Well, his wife showed up with a gold fish net dress with nothing underneath; no slip, no bra, no panties...nada... zero…nothing. I stand corrected. She did have a black garter belt and black nylons on with black heels.

"Have more Champaign and you won't even notice her." I laughed.

"VeHorn, she's coming over here, she likes you sir studly." Gloria giggled.

"Yeah, I see that and she's loaded."

"Oh VeHorn you have such a pretty date, but you have to save a dance for me honey,"

Mrs. Milquetoast slurred.

As she said that she pressed her orbs against my chest. One of her nipples came right through the fish net. Worse than that she had "boob bags" (breast implants) which most men don't like. They are entirely acceptable for medical reasons but not for cosmetic purposes. When she walked behind me she made a quick pass over my lower left cheek. Gloria was laughing.

"You are so James Bond baby...she couldn't control herself."

"Your sharp tongued wit and sarcasm are legendary…but I like that in you." I shot back laughing.

But wait, there's more. Sure enough Mrs. "M" came over to our table, grabbed me out of my chair and led me to the dance floor.

"I'm gonna make you beg for mercy baby," making sure everyone heard her.

The band was well known in the club circuit, especially at the yacht clubs. At the moment we went to the dance floor they were playing a slow holiday jazz number. My dance partner pressed her quim tight against my crotch and started to sway.

"Hey... don't fall...Let's dance a fast one."

"Yeah, I wanna see you move...hey band play us a hot one," she yelled.

By now she had everyone's attention. It was apparent that dirty dancing was her For'te...or maybe not...maybe she had another talent...but I certainly wasn't interested in finding out. Without missing a beat, Mrs. "M" picked up somebody's drink from a table.

"Stop the music... stop the music..." she loudly told the band.

The band did as they were told, as she stumbled up to the stage drink in hand and grabbed the microphone. I sat down at my table with Gloria as fast as I could.

"I want to propose a toast... everybody raise yer glasses," she roared into the mic.

The room was dead silent.. .all the glasses were raised...you could feel the quiet anticipation. The back lighting on the stage glowed right through her fish net dress leaving nothing to the imagination.

"There are two kinds of women in the world, spitters and swallow-ers... here's to swallowers!" She blasted into the microphone as she took a big slug of her drink.

The silence that followed was foreboding. The vice president's face was twisted with anger. All eyes were on him to see what would happen next. No one was Laughing... except for one person. I was laughing so hard I nearly fell off of my chair. "Shhh, VeHom, shhhh you'll get fired," Gloria whispered.

She didn't know that he couldn't fire me so I poured gasoline on the fire. (note: for the sake of this scene we will call him Edward not his name but he really hated to have a " Y" or an "i.e." added to his name). I looked right at the big stuffed shirt.

"Go ahead Eddie, laugh…that was funny as hell." I said.

Mrs. "M" left the stage and the band started playing "Jingle Bells." Somehow that struck me as being funny and I laughed all the harder. Eddie kept looking daggers at me. Now he hated me even more.

"I agree with you about breast implants, I know a few girls who got them….it's really a bad idea."

"Why is that?" I asked.

"The doctors don't tell you that almost all of your nipple sensitivity is lost and won't come back and that your breasts are always cold to the touch…it's so unfair…one girl I know went into depression," Gloria answered.

"Yeah, it's more than that…I met this girl when she was thirty nine… she already had those damn things…she got regular mammograms but because of those plastic boobs the docs missed a malignant nodule...she went through hell and was dead by forty one."

"Oh, that is so sad."

"I went to her funeral...her nineteen year old son came home from the Navy to be there."

"I would never have it done...I went with a guy who tried to talk me into it and said he would pay to have it done... that really made me mad...I told him if he didn't like me the way I was then he could go to hell...I never saw him again."

"Good for you...a lot of women get it done because their boyfriends want it... then the guy is gone and she's never the same...sometimes mutilated."

I changed the subject because it was getting too intense. We spent the night together and I saw her until the spring when she was transferred to New York. We visited a few times after that but life went on. Friends may come and friends may go but enemies last forever. We did remain friends.

"Hey VeHorn," it was Phillips voice on the phone, "the party' s over baby, move all of your things out on Saturday so nobody sees you... take everything...papers, records computers...the works...I'll tell you more next week."

It was Friday morning before a summer three day week end. Most of the brokers would be gone by noon. Virtually no one would be in the office tomorrow. A national holiday was the perfect time to catch people unaware.

"Going out of town this week end Horney?" Mr. Milquetoast asked.

"I really haven't made any plans."

"Well my wife and I are having a private party Sunday night before the holiday; we'd like to have you come over about eight."

I said okay and I almost knew what was going to happen. He never called me Horney so it had to be his wife's idea. Cuckold was the term that came to mind. I went to the "Private" party which turned out to be quite a swinger's group. Mrs. "M" and her hubby were members in what I would say was "good standing." There were several single women but only one single man, and I was the one.

"Oh baby I'm so glad you could make it," she said handing me a martini, "shaken not stirred James Bond."

'Thank you for that," I smiled.

"You are my James Bond tonight," she whispered as her tongue licked the top lip.

I would guess her to be about mid forties and not really bad looking. Of course she was always at the top of her game in makeup and fashion. This night she really out did herself. A sheer red chiffon robe with feathers around the neck matched her red garter belt and nylons. She wore red bedroom heels with feathers that matched her outfit.

"Follow me." She demanded.

She hurriedly walked down a long hall in her home with me in tow. When we got to the end of the hall she opened the master bedroom door. As soon as we walked in she closed and locked the bedroom door. A red hue filled the room as the lighting reflected on what appeared to be a man sitting on a chair at the foot of the king sized bed.

"All right you little worthless bastard I'm going to show you how a real man fucks me...you want to watch don't you...you want to see his cock ram into my cunt...don't you... answer me you little pricked pussy."

My martini buzz was gone. There sat Mr. Milquetoast naked on a straight backed dining room chair with his legs tied around each one of the chair legs and his hands tied behind him. He had a ball gag over his mouth which allowed him to make noise but not speak. She was right he did have a mini dick, but it was hard and throbbing anticipating the show.

"Sit on the bed."

Having said that she dropped her robe to the floor and got on her knees in front of me. After my shoes were removed I stood up as she removed my slacks and shorts. My shirt was slid up over my head and thrown across the room.

"Get on your knees sideways in front of the chair."

The whole scene must have been practiced. I was now kneeling on the bed with him on the chair to my left side. She got on her knees on the bed directly in front of me and leaned down.

"You want to see me suck another man's cock don' t you?"

"U h...Uh... Uh..."was all he could utter with the ball gag.

"Louder you little wimp... you want to see me lick his balls long and slow don't you?

"Uh...Uh.. .Uh...Uh... "he responded louder than before as his little prick throbbed.

She then followed through first putting her mouth over my cock sticking it back and forth all the way down her throat... all the while running her finger nails lightly back and forth over my balls.

"Eeeee... Eeeee... Eeeee... Eeee" he whined excitedly.

He was like a kid on Christmas morning that can't wait to open his next gift. Each one was more fun than the last. This gift was still wrapped with the red heels, nylons and garter belt all in tact. Her perfume was highly erotic. Way better than the scent of pine. I was suddenly to have a close encounter with her sensuous perfume. It was her show and she was totally in control.

"Lay on your back."

I lay on my back with my head parallel and centered with the chair. At that point she straddled my face. The freshly shaved sexual scent of her mons blended perfectly with her perfume. My cock shuddered when she pushed her vag lips over my mouth as her warm cream slid over my tongue. I was slowly licking her clit up and down. She began to make low moans.

"Oh baby he knows how to do it... oh my god... oh my god," she squealed.

After that she got up and told me to get behind her as she got on her knees. Her inner thighs were all wet. She then grabbed my cock and stuck it in her quim. I started to pump her.

"His cock feels so hot in me... I love it baby... turns you on doesn't it... pump me pump me."

"Eeee... Eeee... Eeee.. .Uh... Uh...Uh... " he was sounding over and over.

Her body heaved and she let out a shriek. I could feel her inside squeeze around my cock. She squirted hard...at the same time she reached out and grabbed his little prick she jerked it once he did a high whine and squirted in the air.

After the encounter she untied him and fixed us a drink from the bar in the bedroom. "I presume that you will say nothing."

"You can be assured that the answer is absolutely not... besides what would I gain... we might get together again sometime."

"I want you to know that I never fool around behind my husband's back. We either do it together or not at all... sometimes people get the wrong idea and want to see me alone. We don't do that."

"I would prefer it that way since I don't get involved with married women...you two have an understanding and that's fine with me."

We did get together a number of times after that. They introduced me to their swinger friends and to the club. Like other tourists swingers come to Florida for a vacation for sun and fun...mostly for the fun.

Mr. " M" was quiet as usual. She let me know that she was the boss and he did say that's how he liked it. He was a highly successful broker and an honest one as well. In fact he was one of the few that wound up with no legal problems.

It was too early Tuesday morning, the first day after a three day national holiday when the phone rang.

"You son of a bitch... you rotten piece of..." 'Eddie' was cursing me out.

During the course of the one sided conversation which included expletives from a foreign language which I believed to be Eastern European his secretary interrupted.

"Mr. (last name *(NIA)*, Mr. *(NIA)* the U.S. Marshalls and the SEC are here we have to get out..."

At that point he hung up the phone, and of course he thought that I knew this was going to happen. I really didn't know this was going to occur. I was only told to get out ASAP quietly on the prior Saturday. It was all good.

The Federal Marshalls removed everyone from the building and retained them in the parking lot while they removed all records and computers. They even searched all of the purses, briefcases and cars. These guys probably had warrants to get into your panties.

I just couldn't pass up the opportunity to gloat. I drove up to the office where everyone was standing outside and waved at them from my car. I was shocked no; make that amazed that my former colleagues would greet me back with single finger salutes.

We thought at that time that the era of junk bonds was over and that now Wall Street would clean up its act. The reader knows better. The next debacle was all about derivatives, liar loans, cancelling the Glass Stiegel Act and generally putting the foxes in the hen house.

Not to mention the liars war, Iraq, with its buckets of blood and trillions of dollars lost. The liars club, known more commonly as the neo conservatives, lied us into a quagmire with consequences yet to be discovered.

The cost of all of these outrages has nearly brought America to its knees. Were we really surprised to see that bastion of "free market forces" have a sudden epiphany to believe in socialism? Wall Street's hogs went sobbing to the Feds so they could slop at the public trough or go belly up. Funny how a social safety net can keep a society stable. Tell that to the new owner of the Wall Street Journal, Rupert Murdoch, who beats the drum loudly for "free market forces." It was really a pleasure to not renew my subscription in what now has become just another conservative rag.

CHAPTER 20

———◆———

THE SCENT OF GARLIC AND oregano drifted through the traffic noise and distant sirens. Autumn in New York was even better than described in the song. Thanksgiving would be here soon with the Macy's parade. Holiday lights, decorations and music seemed to make the city glow.

I schlepped through the financial services district scheduling appointments or leaving resumes. I was staying with a college friend who already worked for a Wall Street firm.

"Hey buddy you've been here for two weeks, you need a break." Gordian smiled as he leaned back in the love seat sipping a martini.

He and his roommate Ralph shared a swanky apartment in Manhattan. The superb decor included some early original paintings by contemporary artists... the low background music was always jazz. Gordian and Ralph worked at the same firm and had been a couple for about five years. They were highly sophisticated and very aware that they were living the good life.

"We have a pitcher of martinis ready, so enjoy...shaken not stirred right Ralph...You know VeHom is such a bitch for James Bond," Gordian scoffed then they both laughed.

"We're having a party in your honor on Saturday night... some key people you'll want to meet... aaaand just for you our hetero friend some top female models...just stick close to them so our gay friends will know you' re straight...we' ll tell them in advance you're not a convert but that you're cool ... but you know, boys will be girls." Ralph said, always having fun with this.

These guys were great and they knew how to party. We attended top Broadway cast parties such as Camelot and West Side Story. I was duly impressed. My goal was to get a job on Wall Street; I could get very used to this.

"You're enrolled in a gentleman's seminar... don't get nervous...It's pricey, lasts two days...and It's paid for."

"Gordian, if you think I need it I'll pay for it."

"Oh please...I'm not trying to prostitute you...If you're going to live here there are a few things you need to know...just to put more class in your act... not that you don' t already have class...a few finishing touches is all... just think of it as finishing school." He had a serious tone in his voice.

The universal motivators, money and sex, are always at the bottom of any venture. This seminar offered both. In fact, the title was simply "A Gentleman's Seminar" but the how of monetary and sexual gain was far more subtle...far more effective.

The audience was made up of Wall Street types...cookie cutter copies of each other. The three piece suit was in fashion, with wide ties and lapels. The gold pen of a particular brand was a must, as was a leather valise. About eighty of us sat four to a table facing a raised stage. The podium had a microphone with two plush chairs one on either side of the lectern.

The chandelier lights in this upscale New York hotel dimmed as spotlights were lit to illuminate each table. A hush fell over the audience as a stately brunette walked like a model from stage left to the speaker's stand. Her white blouse was covered by a closed blue business blazer which smoothed easily over the hips of her business length matching blue blazer skirt. Navy blue nylons enhanced her slender legs which were eased into high fashion heels. With long dark hair that was tightly pinned up and black rimmed glasses she had the look of a very sexy librarian.

"Good morning gentlemen." A low voice with a slight French accent greeted the group. "My name is Collette Bideaux Biltmore and I am your professor... I have created this seminar and presented it internationally...there are special presentations however for Americans."

Ms. Biltmore went on to explain that she was from Quebec that her father was American and her mother was French. She was a handsome woman who appeared to be in her early forties. By handsome, I mean sharper features but with a dazzling smile and a dimple on her right cheek. Collette was a class act and seemed very proper...so proper in fact that her next statements absolutely floored everyone.

"The rules are we will have no snickering or inappropriate behavior, or I will have security remove you permanently. I will now present my credentials."

Her right hand adjusted her eye glasses slightly while a brief smile crossed her lips. She stepped out from behind the podium and stood in front of it holding the microphone.

" I am substantially more than qualified to present these semi-nars...you see I have been a five thousand dollar per night escort travelling throughout the world.. .In a very short time I started one of the most if not the most successful international escort services ever... having a highly influential client base there were never any legal problems. I left the business nearly seven years ago."

The audience was stunned. No wonder she first noted that any ' inappropriateness' would result in expulsion. Only the silent echo of her words could be heard in our minds. If shock is the mother of attentiveness... she had our complete concentration...which became even more intense as she let her hair down and removed her dark rimmed glasses.

"From London to Paris...New York to Las Vegas...I have thoroughly studied the art and science of culture. You will learn about din-ing, fashion, hygiene...yes, hygiene.. .art, music, dancing, drinking, investing, and even gambling...even so I'm not sure how much of a difference there is between those two. I will not make James Bonds of you but at least you will be able to tastefully frequent the clubs he attends without embarrassing yourselves."

An easy transition was made from subject to subject with a sylla-bus hand out that was simple but detailed. She would walk back and forth across the stage, sometimes sitting on one of the plush chairs... all the while holding the microphone or clipping it to the waist of her now open blazer. Frequently she would refer to the slide screen that was to the left of the stage. The opening subject was about communicating.

"Speaking English with an understandable foreign accent is fine... How you talk speaks volumes about you...Including your vocabu-lary and education. Speaking English with a regional accent will not get you to the place you wish to be. In England a cockney accent doesn't get it... the same goes in the U.S. for southern, and other accents that place you in a certain socio economic class." Biltmore said in a matter of fact fashion.

She could be really brutal...saying that if you lived in this country all of your life and couldn't or wouldn't speak at least business English then go back to school and study it. Of course she was right especially if your goal was to be in the upper tier of society or at least business.

I later discovered that Ms. Collette Bideaux Biltmore's mother's maiden name was Bideaux. Her father was a highly successful international banker. She was bilingual of course as are most Canadians in both French and English. It was not surprising to learn that Collette had a master's degree in social science. Her life style was by choice after having been jilted by a very wealthy well known and married American.

"When we started this morning with Aristotle's ' Know Thy Self ...I want to add love thy self... because if you don't then you cannot love another...I believe the fact that you' re here says that you at least like your selves."

I am usually underwhelmed, but that was not the case with Collette. It wasn't just her worldliness, or even her sexually sophisticated image. It was the whole package... including her obviously classical education.

"The best advice I can give you about men's fashions is the advice that Polonius gave to his son Laertes...'costly thy habit as thy purse may buy, but not expressed in fancy... rich... but not gaudy... for the apparel often proclaims the man' ... in today's words quite simply, the clothes makes the man... so don't be fancy or gaudy." She smiled while reading the quote.

The basics were all mentioned...just as Technya (Tech) had taught me... fit, selection, color, understated...good taste above all else. Good men's magazines were suggested including Playboy since their ads showed the current styles.

She said her best investment advice came from her father who told her to buy blue chip stocks and hold. His other recommendation was to buy into the S&P five hundred and hold. If you want to buy a flyer just remember to cut your losses.

The seminar continued. She announced on the first day that the final segments were about hygiene...with the best of the best for last... namely... S-E-X. Collette started in a tutorial way and then became a tad sarcastic. She didn't pull any punches.

"Gentlemen, the truth is that you are not a gaggle of hygiene geniuses...in my line of work I have been disgusted with men and women who fail the basics of being clean. Do you remember when mom or grandma always told you to wear clean undies? If you clean yourself properly in the first place you won't have a problem with that in the second place." She protested; rolling her eyes.

The seminar attendant appeared on stage with a low table and placed it to her right side. A roll of bathroom tissue and two plastic bottles, one small, and one large sat on table top.

"There is nothing more disgusting or a greater turn off for men or women than the issue of dirty underwear."

At that point she picked up the roll of bathroom tissue and held it up high...turning to each side of the audience making sure they saw it.

"You know of course that women use this when they urinate. I am telling you to do the same thing...dripping the last few drops of pee in your underwear makes you stink like stale urine and causes yellow stains. You cannot shake it all off...use this (she held up the bath tissue)... remember, the job isn't over til the paperwork is through."

There was not a snicker to be heard... not a word. She then turned around and picked up one of the plastic bottles while still holding the tissue roll in her hand.

"There is no way that you can clean yourself with tissue only. I would hope that all women already know this, but they don't, and most men don't have a clue. In Europe bathrooms are equipped with a bidet which is a spray of water which aids in cleansing...that's better but not good enough."

I knew what was coming next because my grandmother had taught me in no uncertain terms that short of a bristle brush... which she threatened to use if I had anything but clean underwear... lotion was the answer.

"This is baby lotion, and this is bathroom tissue." She said holding each in either hand.

Ms. Biltmore proceeded to give intricate instructions on how to use this marvelous method of hers to clean ones backside. The directions included lotion on tissue to clean the outside then wrapping a finger in the paper and, applying lotion to clean the inside. It was really quite simple and informative. After the seminar a lot of guys commented among themselves that they never knew and wished someone had told them before.

"Mom used baby lotion on you when she changed your nappy (diaper)…paper alone will not work…so if you want to avoid smelling like a sewer always use lotion…the large bottle for home use and the small bottle put into your briefcase or pocket for other times."

Guys were actually taking notes…like you couldn't remember this beautiful woman at this seminar instructing you about the finer points of hygiene without taking notes? That was laughable but I didn't laugh….I truly believe she would have had me removed.

Besides the best part…sex…was about to be presented.

"I always insist. .. and I tell my escorts to do the same…that a man showers before sex. In addition, there are only two types of men who have sex without condoms…those that have had STD…or still have…and those who will have STD… and by the way… remember… herpes is a gift that keeps on giving."

Her way of having you remember the more salient points of her seminar included subtle humor and vivid mental nightmare images of herpes blisters and green gonorrhea goo dripping from the urethra. As they say on television commercials…'but wait, there's more.'

"Anal sex is okay if both partners agree…that's never been a turn on for me, but some women do like it as do some men. If you have anal sex wear a condom…don' t go bare back. Here's why…a number of urologists say if you have anal sex without condoms it's possible that you' ll wind up with E-Coli bacteria in your prostate gland. If that's the case the only thing your penis is good for then is to pee out of."

The sexology did not stop there. A sort of rating system was introduced regarding sex and where you stood on the social scale. This was not a surprise, but it was the first time I had ever heard someone categorize people sexually based on choices. It was a sexual profile that only her expertise could develop.

"I never hire an escort with breast implants not only because virtually all nipple sensitivity is lost but most men get bored with them. I tell both men and women to avoid getting body piercings and tattoos because they lower your social value. Even a small Rose tattoo is not acceptable. I attended a conference of plastic surgeons who say their biggest cosmetic business now is to remove both breast implants and tattoos."

Collette was sympathetic for women who needed breast implants for medical reasons such as cancer. She was highly critical however of women who got implants for cosmetic reasons.

"If my escorts get implants they have to leave... even if a boyfriend wants and pays for breast implants... they're gone. All too often the guy dumps them and the girl is left holding the bags, if you will, and she winds up working at a lower cost agency."

"In closing there a few pointers...I' ll share... I've told my escorts that they must always shave their pubic hair... that's good advice for guys too since the genitals stay cleaner without hair and it reduces the incidence of lice...it also looks sexier to be shaved... and nobody wants to get hair in their mouths... incidentally, if you want your penis to look bigger shave the hair around it so it' s not hiding behind a bush." She chuckled this time.

The seminar was coming to a close so she opened up the floor for a few questions.

"Does size make a difference?" A chubby chap asked.

"No... since the vagina has nerve sensors within the first three inches. Beyond that the feeling is dull until the pain threshold is felt. After about eight inches most women will feel discomfort and even pain if the uterus is hit. We always had rubber donuts available for longer sized men to slide down the penis base to prevent full insertion... and if a personal lubricant is needed don't use a packaged vaginal liquid... use extra virgin olive oil...no chemical irritations and olive oil tastes better."

"What about facial hair?"

"I see you have a goatee and a mustache... most women don't like facial hair or whisker stubble during oral sex...rub that mess of facial hair on tender skin...and the whisker burns will turn the lady off. I don't know who thought that beard stubble was so sexy... it is n't... of course if you don't like oral sex then keep the mustaches, beards and stubble...I' m sure your dog won't mind."

Ms. Biltmore had mastered the art of sarcastic humor, and with that she let us know her point of view. That's why we came to the seminar...for the same reason that anyone would attend a university... to learn a different perspective from an expert in her field.

"What about body hair...I had a girlfriend who wanted me to get it removed."

"I'd put that in the same category as a man who insists that his girlfriend get implants... drop her like a bad habit...some women love body hair on a man, especially on the chest... we had a blonde haired client whose chest hair formed a natural path right down to his penis. All the escorts thought that was sexy...what can I say, some women like it some don't... but you'll never have a woman's respect if she can intimidate you into removing your body hair... or in any other way."

Colette stayed to sign her book. I purchased one, waited, and then walked last up to the signing table.

"I' m glad I attended your seminar...it was unique." I said with a sly smile.

"Oh," she said smiling back, "I noticed that you had pretty impressive eye contact."

"Well, I do have ulterior motives...a couple friends of mine are throwing a party for an off Broadway cast tonight...you know the type, artists, models, and other creatures."

"Mmmmm... well, I really like your indirect approach." She laughed..."Okay...be in the lobby at seven."

Her red sheath dress with slight side slits caught the attention of everyone in the lobby, especially me. A black snake skin bag with matching heels gave the hint of a slithering effect as she moved toward me.

"Hi...I'm not surprised...you look absolutely dazzling." Was about all I could say.

"Thanks...you look very sharp yourself...such a stunning couple... we'll make a grand entrance." She warmly smiled making her dimple deepen.

Collette knew how to make a man feel good about himself. She placed her arm under mine and gave a squeeze. A light autumn breeze fluffed up her long dark wavy hair just enough for the bright outside hotel lights to reflect off her single diamond earrings. A yellow gold chain around her neck held a larger single diamond. As she slipped into the taxi's back seat the right slit in her dress raised a little showing her dark thigh top nylons. A black sparkled woven wrap wound through her elbows and over the left bare shoulder.

"Who are you?" She asked.

"Very good, just like in your seminar... know thyself."

"I never ask a man that unless I'm interested...usually I just feed their egos...I'd like to know more about you...even though a lot guys in that room would love to have asked me for a date...you had the balls to do it." Collette said with a quiet laugh.

We learned more about each other on the way to my friend's party. She let me know that she was bi and was I okay with that.

"I' m fine with that, in fact maybe we can get together there with a lady we both like." I said.

"I'm surprised...you're pretty sophisticated for a guy of twenty four...I like that...we'll find somebody." She said as she came closer.

Collette's left hand was now on my right cheek as she pulled my head slowly closer to hers and gently pressed her lips on mine. Her tongue slipped into my mouth and then inside between my lips and teeth...slowly, sensually circling first the top lip and then the bottom lip. I was becoming aroused, and then the taxi stopped.

"I thought we would never make it out of the cab." I said laughingly as we walked hand in hand.

We were alone in the apartment building elevator. Collette turned her body toward me pressing against my cock. She then placed her left hand on it and gently squeezed until it was straight up. The elevator stopped. I was beginning to feel like an elevator, first the taxi and now this.

"Paul, it pays to advertise. .. some of the lady crotch watchers will get turned on to us if they see you are turned on," she giggled.

The bell hadn't stopped ringing when Ralph opened the door. A flood of red and blue hues shown into the hallway as a scent mixed with perfumes, smoke, alcohol and incense wafted out. The low sound of midnight jazz and conversations filled the air.

"Oh my God, he even has a James Bond girl...come in...what is your name...my lord you look ravishing...let me take your wrap...I may even slip it on... Gordian your pupil is here."

If nothing else Ralph was not only entertaining, but he really knew how to entertain. Artists, models, equity actors, and always musicians and all were wrangling for invitations to Gordian and Ralph's parties. Of course the upside for them was comp tickets to plays, concerts, art shows and the parties that followed. Gordian came over to meet Collette.

"Paul, you rascal... you brought the seminar professor...Collette isn't it...I saw your photo...so Paul, how was this teach-in?" Asked Gordian, while holding his drink and beaming.

"As profoundly interesting as is the instructor," I said smiling while looking into Collette' s eyes.

"Great answer...what a smooth operator...let's get you two some libations...oh yes, and you'll find that the hors d' oeuvres are scrumptious...be careful Collette... I already saw some guys fantasizing about him...I think he's just too hetero for his own good." Gordian said as he laughed.

"Nothing personal, but I'm glad to hear that...he seems pretty cool about everything." She replied.

We did the martini thing...she insisted on ' shaken not stirred' since Ralph had called her a James Bond girl. She was into astrology explaining some character types and who she got along with.

"Did you know that Shakespeare used astrology for character types...Falstaff is the classic Taurus while Hamlet, the prince of indecision, is definitely a Libra... VeHorn, what are you?" She asked.

"Surprise, surprise... I happened to have had a grand aunt that did astrological readings...she told me that I am an Aires with a Scorpio rising sign and a Scorpio moon."

"Scary, really scary...that means you're not nice but you are fun... not a person to cross...ever...you will get even...but you are loyal to a fault... oh yeah the Aires part gives you the energy to do what the Scorpio is always thinking about." She said with that sly smile of hers.

"And what is that?"

"You act as if you didn't know... sex of course... I mean really... that's true." She laughed.

"Okay Ms. Bideuax just what is your zodiac sign?"

"Capricorn, through and through...your shirt' s monogrammed with PRV as in perv... what does that stand for, pervert?"

"Absolutely... somebody has to be... no, it means Paul Robert VeHorn... PRV... not only have I been called perv in school but also Horny instead of VeHorn...but you can call me whatever."

We both were feeling no pain as we worked on our third martini. A very slender model looked our way several times and smiled.

"Okay, I'll call you whatever... no, I like Horny…and perv.. .I'll call you both which ever fits at the time...I'll tell you a secret...I have a name that only my closest girl friends know and can call me...only in private...I'll tell you but you can only call me that in private... want to hear it?" She asked with a slight slur.

"Of course I want to hear it."

"Clit...short for Collette...clit...heh heh...you like it?"

"I love it...but showing is better than telling." I laughed.

She said she liked my sense of humor...at that point we both agreed to eat something and to back off on the martinis. I asked if she noticed the young model that has glanced at us.

"Not only did I notice her... but I can tell she is bi and she's our date for later tonight...let's eat something and go talk to her." Collette's voice had an almost sinister tone to it.

The slender body undulating in an irregular hemmed dress of shimmering blue and silver was obviously that of a top model. The blue highlights of her short dark hair which waved over one eye matched the deep blue color of her eyes. As we walked over to meet her, she turned to us with a slight almost boyish smile.

"Hi, if you're not a fashion model already you ought to be." Collette said in a low sexy voice.

"Why thank you...my name is Yvonne." She smiled putting her hand out.

'My name is Collette and this is my date, Paul...we were admiring you from afar.. .I love the blue blends in your dress and even your hair...don't tell me your dress designer...I will just turn green." Collette laughed.

She was doing a great job of schmoozing. I could tell by her body language that Yvonne knew the script. After some more small talk the ladies decided to go to the rest room. Her silver nylons shimmered as she and Collette walked together. Both of them were less than steady walking in their heels...the alcohol was taking its toll. They seemed to be gone longer than usual. .. when they returned Yvonne had a small lipstick smudge on the comer of her mouth. Collette motioned to her and Yvonne quickly rubbed her left forefinger over it.

"Paul, we're all going to my place I'll have room service bring in something to eat...we'll have drinks, and spend the evening together...just the three of us." That sly smile of Collette's was showing again.

"I hope that's okay with you Paul." Yvonne said insecurely.

"I couldn't be happier...it's my pleasure." I said.

Yvonne then pulled me close with her mouth to my ear... in almost a whisper...said, "I know I'm really slender and I'm flat on top... you're good with that?"

"To me that is totally erotic, and you are totally erotic." I assured her.

"You are so sweet." She said caressing my head and kissing me.

We left the party and arrived at Collette's hotel. She had a large two room suite with two baths. Room service brought a dozen small single serve quiche shrimp pies and four bottles of chilled Champaign. After room service left Collette dimmed the lights; then generously sprinkled what appeared to be oregano on the tops of the quiche. Of course it was high grade marijuana; not oregano.

"The quiche is catching up with me...I feel really smooth." I said, smiling.

"We're going to the master bath perv...better get ready." Collette laughed.

I went to the smaller bath and showered for what seemed like hours. Finally, wrapped in a towel I went back into the living room and had another quiche with more Champaign. I was feeling no pain when suddenly both girls entered the room together. They looked like a wet dream come true.

"You like what you see?" Yvonne asked.

They were both freshly showered and shaved smooth. Yvonne wore what I thought earlier were silver nylons. Only it was better... the nylons were really open crotch panty hose. Her silver blue heels were just high enough to elevate the perfectly oval cheeks of her slim derriere. Collette was now wearing a red and black garter belt with red nylons. Four inch spike heels made her legs look longer and she seemed much taller. She had some sex toys in her hand which she laid down. As they sat down next to me on either side, Clit slipped my towel open.

"Do I like what I see... paradise...just paradise". Was all I could say.

Two tongues slowly, deliberately slide up my neck while Clit's hand is rubbing my right nipple and Yvonne's fingers are gently pinching my left nipple. Yvonne is on my left side; she turns my head and faces me as her tongue drifts across my mouth and into my lips. As she is kissing me Collette presses her own left nipple into my mouth. Yvonne then removed her tongue and pressed her right nipple into my mouth. I move my hands to each of their bare nipples and squeeze and tease their nipples with my fingers while gently biting their nipples which the girls are pressing harder into my mouth.

Collette pulls her left nipple out of my mouth then trails her right hand down the right side of my body methodically tickling along the way until her hand stops at my right inner thigh. She lightly brushes my now tight balls with her hand as she descends from the couch and gets on her knees. Yvonne removes her nipple from my mouth and slips her tongue between my lips...then she moves her tongue to my neck and slides her mouth down my left side all the while darting her tongue in and out as she unhurriedly gets lower. At first I feel Yvonne's tongue slightly licking the left side of my balls... then I feel Collette's tongue on the right side...I look down and they kiss each other as they take turns licking my balls and then kissing again. My throbbing cock is so hard that I fully expect to find stretch marks on it after this sex fest. As both wet tongues begin to run up my quivering penis shaft and under the now purple ridge of my stiff cock I start to moan.

" Oh my god... mmmmm....mmmmm....ooooh," were my only sounds. " Get on your knees Yvonne." Clit said sternly.

As I looked down from my seat on the couch I saw Yvonne on her knees between my open legs. Collette was standing behind her with a strap on dildo... then she got on her knees behind Yvonne. She was definitely in command.

"Suck his cock bitch." Clit demanded.

I could feel the head of my cock slide over Yvonne's moist lips... then the shaft being sucked into her warm wet mouth. One of her hands was caressing my balls while the fingers of the other lightly clawed them. Yvonne tensed up... Clit had just penetrated her quim with the dildo.

"Mmmmm... Mmmmm... Mmmmm." Yvonne kept moaning while sucking my hot rod.

Collette would pull the dildo all the way out and stick it in again, over and over. Each time Yvonne would tense up, moan, and suck harder. It was all I could do to keep from blasting my cock cream down her throat. Clit was wildly slapping Yvonne's ass the whole time while calling her a bitch and telling her to suck that cock harder.

"Lay down on the floor perv." Collette ordered.

Yvonne scooted back as I laid the towel down on the floor and got on my back. The pressure on my cock eased off for only a moment. Clit took off the dildo in an instant... squatted over my cock... and stuck it in.

"Sit on his face bitch...squirt your hot twat cream in his mouth." Collette all but yelled.

A warm primal musky cream surged into my mouth as I heard Yvonne's orgasmic squeals echo in my ears. The sweet pungent aroma and taste of her womanly essence was exquisite. All the while Collette was pumping and pumping my cock with her quim. She was insatiable.

"Aaaaaaaaaah... oh my god....yeeeeeeeee... oh... oh... oh." Collette was having a violent orgasm.

Her vaginal walls squeezed together over and over gripping my cock like a vice. Both Clit and I were overwhelmed at once with deep intense screaming orgasms.

We virtually all passed out for a couple hours. We were wasted. Around four AM we got into the King sized bed in the master bedroom. I made it with each of them during the night as we would wake up. Something different...I was on top.

"Guys we'll have some breakfast sent up then I have a plane to catch. We have to get together and do that again sometime." Collette yawned.

We managed to get up, shower, and have breakfast in the room together. We kept the room darkened. I think we all knew 'that again sometime' would never happen. I did see Yvonne a couple times in Miami. Collette and I wrote a few times. A moment in time to never be repeated... if only we had a video... but life goes on.

CHAPTER 21

———•———

It took a while for my trip to Wall Street to be productive. In the meantime I opened an agency as an independent broker. About ten months passed when I received a call.

"VeHorn and associates," I answered.

"Hi, this is Jim Jameson; I'd like to speak to Paul VeHorn," was the reply.

"Speaking," I said.

"I'd like to come down to have lunch with you tomorrow... you spoke to our company in New York and I want to follow up... pick you up at your office at eleven thirty." He said in a kind of western accent.

"Time out Jim Jameson...first what's this all about and second I have to check my schedule."

"Come on VeHom, no self respecting broker has appointments on Friday afternoon...if you have a tee time cancel it...this is more important." He laughed.

I kind of liked the guy's ballsy approach and I told him as much.

"You know you got a lot of cojones...I like that...you' re right I'm off on Friday afternoon but no tee time tomorrow.. .see you at eleven thirty."

"I know where you are VeHorn...eleven thirty...I'll pick you up in a limo...have a good one." Jamison answered.

Pick me up in a limo I thought. They're trying to make an impression, but that wasn't all. It turned out that he came down in a corporate jet...picked me up in a cushy long Cadillac limo and drove to a well known country club for lunch. Ever meet someone you like right away? Well, that was Jameson. He had a great sense of humor and a searing gaze that seemed to see right through any phoniness. We had a private room with our own waitress.

"Bring us two martinis... how do you like yours VeHorn?" He liked to use my last name.

"London gin....two olives."

The James Bond martini was the number one drink of the decade... shaken not stirred of course... except in Miami where the Cuba Libra was numero uno. I could see that this was going to be a three martini lunch with hors d' oeuvres. Jameson had it all strategically planned.

"You don't just have beautiful hair; you really know how to enhance your looks with the way you style it." I said to the waitress as she brought our second martini.

"Why thank you so much," she said with a big smile.

As she walked away, I saw Jameson with a big smile; lifting his martini in a toast fashion.

"Well done VeHorn, you really do know how to sell...I'm glad I saw that... nothing crude like you have a great rack...or some damn thing." He smiled.

About half way through the second martini he got serious and told me what he had in mind. When I told him I wasn't interested; he looked at me with that particular gaze of his. He liked to use the word deal.

"Ok here's the deal VeHorn, I'm prepared to make you an offer you can't refuse...you better not because it's my ass if you turn it down...we did a thorough investigation on you... we believe you can get this job done." His voice was low.

Jameson explained that they had eighteen divisions throughout the country and he needed a division manager for the Florida region. He was the executive vice president of marketing at the home office. The decision was made to pull more revenue out of the Florida region.

"Until now, they've given this position to someone in the company who is near retirement...they just go out and play golf or go fishing...well those days are over...this division is eighteenth out of eighteen...in fact it' s on a minus zero base." He frowned.

During the third martini he made me an offer I truly couldn't refuse. I don't know if he was softening me up with the booze or letting himself give me the bottom line offer. We were both pretty well oiled. The waitress returned and I asked for her telephone number...I found out later that she actually gave me her real number...I've gotten a few wrong numbers, but the best one was the number for the coroner's office.

"We better eat something," Jim slurred.

The waitress suggested a large shrimp and lobster salad covered with a warm lobster lemon sauce...by this time we needed more than hors d' oeuvres and we kept the garlic bread sticks coming.

"I want you to meet the CEO on Wednesday, so fly up the day before...I'll have a company limo pick you up at Kennedy then we'll go to dinner and a broad way show...but now by god I want to go to a gentleman's club...I heard the West Coast of Florida has the top clubs in the country." Jim said eagerly.

He was so right. The fame spread when the first super bowl was played on Florida's West Coast. We left the country club then did a sightseeing drive around the area which included the Gulf beaches. We arrived at a top rated gentleman's club at around eight thirty. The cocktail crowd had already gone and the night crowd was coming aboard. This group was made up of the more serious nude dance club aficionados including professional athletes and upper echelon tourists.

"I'm impressed VeHorn, this is no crummy nude dance club... this place is a palace." Jim said as he ogled the ladies.

"I' ll give you the best lap dance you have ever had in your life honey as soon as the show is over." One of the bustier starlets said to him as her natural orbs jiggled.

"Jameson I'm told this is the best there is...I didn't even know that they had a stage and a show.. .I thought it was just pole dancing, lap dancing and VIP rooms." I remarked looking around at the expensive decor.

With a great deal of fanfare the actual show started. The emcee introduced the first of three acts. A tall nude exotic looking lady in high heels walked sensuously out on the stage. Her nails and make up blended perfectly with her skin tone. Her long dark hair style was combed somewhat up and over her left eye. The only thing she was wearing was a python.

"A beautiful woman wearing a nasty snake... and she's dancing with it yet." Jim sounded as if he was totally turned off.

"She has a great body but I'm underwhelmed...I wouldn't touch her after a snake has been slithering all over her...well maybe... after she took a shower," I laughed.

The snake charmer's act at best was weird. The snake wrapped itself around her body until the grand finale when she stood on the stage with her legs together... the snake came out from beneath her quim and then slowly rose up toward her waist looking like an erect schlong.

"You don't see that every day," Jim quipped.

"No, thank god, the next act better be good," I answered.

The next act was funny in a sad way. A well known former porn movie queen we will call her "Queenie" came out on stage wearing very sexy lingerie over a garter belt, nylons and heels. She danced some and then removed her sheer chiffon robe. Of course she was shaved, had breast implants and her navel was pierced with an oversized jewel. When she picked up the microphone she laughed while trying to be funny.

"You' re a great audience and know that a lot of you out there have choked your chickens watching my videos." She said with a coarse voice.

A scattering of laughs came from the audience. She wasn't finished since her main reason for being there was to sell her DVDs complete with a kiss and an autograph. That was special.

"How do you like these bolt-ons?" She asked grabbing her thirty eight ' D' silicone filled but drooping orbs.

I had never quite seen implants take that shape. I later found out that as a woman gets older the breast part with the implant stays the same but the ends beyond the implants along with the nipples droop. It's sort of like holding your hand out straight fingers together and then bending the forward part of your fingers down. I kind of felt sorry for her... and she was trying so hard too.

"Remember after the show I will be at the table in the back just like this to give you a kiss and an autograph when you buy one of my hot DVDs...Love ya guys." Queenie said as she threw a kiss while exiting the stage.

The third and final act was hilarious. I have never seen an act like that before or since. The lady was a ventriloquist...and not just any ventriloquist...you see she had a built in doll. That's right...just what you' re thinking.

"Ladies and gentlemen directly here from Las Vegas are Vicky and Vay Jay... let's give it up for them." The emcee announced.

Vicky was good looking albeit a little on the chunky side but highly talented. She wore thigh tops and heels only. I soon discovered that she couldn't wear a garter belt due to the mechanism that was used to make her lower vagina lip move. Vicky was one really raunchy and funny lady. She came onto the stage and lay down on her left side on a raised table with her head resting on her right hand. Her left hand lay on her hip to operate the bottom lip movement with her left leg raised. Her mons was completely shaved and two large eyes with long lashes and a petite nose were perfectly and professionally drawn above Vay Jay's lips. I never did figure out the mechanics of it except that the lips were hinged and must have had some sort of adhesive (ouch) attached. A monofilament... as in fishing line... was attached and pulled by her left hand.

"What a wild act," was all that Jim could say.

We were laughing like mad men. Her portfolio included outrageous jokes and worse songs. She even had several volunteers come up and pull her string.

" Go ahead, pull the string and say something... ooo...ooo... that feels good do it again," she said to one of the volunteers.

"Hey Jim do you want me to volunteer you," I asked.

"Hell no, I might fall in love...I wonder if I can get my wife to do that."

I told him that I wouldn't go there if l were him. Vicky was a crazy lady...as she left the stage 'Vay Jay' kept talking and making kiss sounds. What an absolutely mind blowing act. We stayed for another couple hours having lap dances. We finally wound up in a VIP room and left around one A.M.

"Okay VeHorn lets roll...we had a night to remember." Jameson said as we got into the limo.

On the way back to his hotel we talked about next week's meeting... He had the driver take me home...The next day I picked up my car at his hotel...Jim had already left.

"VeHorn, how are you...I heard you guys really like ventriloquist shows... you gotta take me there when I come down." The CEO laughed as he greeted me.

Everything was cool at the home office. The interior designer created a business majestic atmosphere. Financial services companies can be opulent. This one had original paintings and statues in the huge reception lobby area. I was duly impressed.

"So what's your strategy VeHorn," suddenly the CEO was all bottom line business.

"I plan to take the first ninety days to do marketing...meet and greet the agencies, the brokers, and the staff." I replied.

"Don't rush...I want you to take one hundred twenty days...by the sixth month I expect to start seeing revenue from that market." the CEO came back.

It is has been said that we hire in our own image. I liked this guy; just like Jameson he was a realist and he was totally pragmatic.

"We came after you because we want a new approach...you're different... to say the least... your majors are communications and psychology...but then you became a successful series seven stock broker, insurance broker and real estate agent," the CEO's voice sounded confident.

Not only had he done his homework, he memorized it as well. Jameson joined in with additional reasons for my hire.

" Look, we are taking a calculated risk here by hiring someone who doesn't' t have an MBA, but we decided we can always hire a bean counter...every one of your department heads has MBAs...but none of them were interviewed for this position." Jameson said.

"We need a people person who knows how to sell without being obnoxious... your region has fifty two employees, one hundred thirty agencies and three hundred brokers... how the hell can it be on a minus zero base." The CEO questioned.

They both said that the days of having semi-retired people from home office being sent to Florida were over. They wanted results and I was going to give it to them. I never realized at that moment what an ecstatic thrill ride was in store for me as a regional director for this financial services company.

CHAPTER 22

———————

I DIVIDED THE REGION INTO three districts... north...middle and south.
I had a marketing person in each one. I really knew how it would
shake out. The northeast area was really South Alabama and at one
time it may have been. That was the Tallahassee area. The other
was really South Georgia; the Jacksonville territory. Florida ought
to really be divided into two states. Everything north of Orlando
is a red state and the rest of the state including Orlando is a blue
state. It will never happen but it's a damned good idea. The way it's
governed now is a cluster fuck...or whatever.

Then there was Miami...the city that cocaine built. It isn't called the
gold coast for nothing. Super popular movies and TV shows were
blockbusters as soon as they came out. The ' Miami Vice' TV series
hit it right on...'Scarface' was another but it was exaggerated. I was
surprised at first when I went to nightclubs in Miami and patrons
were openly using cocaine. I remember going to high class clubs
where in the elegant men's rooms lines of cocaine were spread on
the counters and guys were snorting it. It was never an option for
me, I was into health and moderate drinking was fine with me.

"Listen Mr. V," Malcolm, my Miami marketing rep said..."this is
New York City south and it's a different world than what you're
used to."

Malcolm knew what he was talking about...he grew up in New York City... moved to Miami and graduated from the University of Miami.

"I know you're right...so I'm depending on you to make it happen ASAP." I put a sense of urgency in my voice.

"The first thing I'm going to tell you is to forget about the Cuban owned agencies... they only do business with Cubans...I'm Jewish... they're courteous to me but that's it...look at you...blonde hair, blue eyes, you've got WASP (i.e. White Anglo Saxon Protestant) written all over you."

"Yeah, but my great grandfather was Jewish." I thought out loud.

"So you're going to wear a sign around your neck and schlep through Little Havana? They'll think you're a shmo... oh yeah you better brush up on your Yiddish if you're going to do business here," Malcolm scoffed.

"So Malcolm, I should shmooz them with Yiddish...how about Cuban Yiddish?" I laughed.

" Fardinenzich dem kop (Yiddish, for drive yourself crazy?)... I'm only trying to help you," Malcolm replied.

"Okay, so I'll knock myself out going to the Cuban agencies but I have to try it...which one is the biggest most successful Cuban agency?" I asked.

"So I tried...I'll tell you which one... I have all the stats but I won't go there with you."

Malcolm was serious. He did give me the data on the number one Cuban agency and he had been there. Apparently they were indeed courteous but that was it. He even said he invited the owner for a golf outing which the agency respectfully declined.

I did all of my research the night before, and I arrived at the number one Cuban agency first thing in the morning. Little Havana was a thriving successful section of the city that was exhilarating to be in. As I walked down the sidewalk from the parking garage to the agency the delicious scent of strong Cuban coffee permeated the area. People were sitting outside at the little cafes sipping Cafe con leche (i.e. coffee with milk) as they read Cuban newspapers.

"Good morning I'm Paul VeHorn with (name of the company) I have an appointment to see Mr. Manuela (pseudonym of course)," I smiled.

"Right this way Mr. VeHorn." She said with a slight Cuban accent.

I followed the receptionist...we entered a very large incredibly decorated office...I was offered a seat some distance away from the huge main ornate desk which was obviously the owners. He sat behind his desk facing two half circles of four designer chairs on either side. His staff managers were sitting on the chairs... everyone was speaking in Spanish...rapidly. I sat there for about fifteen minutes admiring the original art works and statuary that was tastefully presented in this the owner's office. When the eight staff members left Mr. Manuela motioned me to come forward and put his hand out as if to say sit down. I sat down on the chair closest to his right while he swiveled his char around to face me.

"Mr. VeHorn would you like a cup of our very famous Cuban Cafe con leche?" He asked in English.

I thanked him and said of course I would. A low coffee table made of driftwood with a plate glass top was sitting in the center of the two half circles of chairs. The receptionist brought in a cup for each of us. We both had a sip then sat our cups into the saucers. At that point Mr. Manuela leaned back in his chair, put his elbows on the chair arms and placed the finger tips of each hand against the other.

"Of course Mr. VeHorn, you are bi-lingual?" He frowned.

"Yes, Mr. Manuela I am," was my straight faced reply.

Manuela then said something in rapid Spanish...I replied not quite as rapidly in German. I spoke German thanks to my grandparents until I was about five years old and after that I sounded like a famous weight lifter ex-governor from California. Manuela looked stunned as he dropped his hands and rolled his chair to the left side of his desk. He pressed the intercom button...he started speaking in English.

"I want everyone in the building into my office now!" His voice was loud and commanding.

I was waiting for a dozen or so... at least... of huge Cuban bouncers to throw my seemingly non respectful ass out the door and onto the street. But no...not this time at least. All and I do mean all, of the employees gathered in his office.

"I want you to know that we are all arrogant...we assume... do you know what assume means...it means to make an ass of you and me...I must admit that today I was wrong...I asked Mr. VeHorn if he was bi-lingual...he said yes...so I speak to him in Spanish and he speaks back to me in German." Manuela's voice was emphatic.

I had to admire this man's sincerity... he sounded almost heroic... almost King Henry the Fifth... as in a 'we band of brothers' moment. I could tell that his people both loved him and were loyal to him. I was soon to find out just why.

"So, Mr. VeHorn, your first language was German?" He asked.

"Yes sir it was German." I respectfully replied.

"So you see we must never do this... we are never going to do this... there are other people in this world...in this country...they deserve the same respect that we want." He instructed.

At that point I said nothing. I later discovered that he saw himself in a nearly godfather role in the Cuban community, but not in a bad sense. He was the 'go to' person for anyone who wanted to curry favor in Little Havana. Every politician who was running for election would make a pilgrimage to his domain.

"Mr. VeHorn...you will cancel all of your appointments from noon for the rest of the day. I am taking you with my staff to the finest Cuban restaurant...you will have the opportunity to see Cuba...all the music all the passion all the dancing." He had a thrill in his voice.

Indeed he showed me the essence of Cuban culture. Every course that was served was something different for me...plantains... Cuban bread.. .trout le russe... all with the background music of a live Spanish guitarist. Periodically Flamenco dancers would perform. Nearly four hours had passed. He ordered Napoleonic Congnac.

"I think you have never had a Cuban cigar," he laughed, "don't worry, Bebe Rebozo enjoyed them with Nixon, like everything else they're only legal for the special people."

We had left the restaurant and arrived back at his office. He committed to doing business with me. He was a prince of a man who earned my respect. I'm usually underwhelmed with my fellow man, but Mr. Manuela had my deepest admiration. Unfortunately he passed away about a dozen years after that... he always kept his word. When he was terminally ill he called and told me he would like to share stories with me again. He made me promise that I would attend his funeral saying that it would be the most magnificent funeral I would ever attend. I kept my promise...it was a tremendous funeral...a show that I know he not only directed, but that he was the leading man.

"How about if I have my marketing man Malcolm set up a golf date with us," I asked before leaving his office.

"Oh, Pablo I don't play golf! Got too good at it," he smiled, "Now if you really want to go someplace we will go to Aruba for deep sea fishing...Just like Papa Hemingway." He said seriously.

"Ok Let's do it: I've never gone after Marlin before."

And do it we did... the following October was perfect for deep sea fishing. We took Jim Jameson, the marketing V.P., Malcolm, along with us. Manuela caught the biggest Marlin. The whole bill was on the corporate expense account, but the yield on that investment was well worth it; Manuela's agency became one of the top producers.

"Well how did it go with Manuela, did they throw you out on your ass?" Malcolm asked

I told Malcolm to meet me for drinks. I explained to him how it went, and he was shocked.

"You have some cajones...I can't believe the chutzpeh you got... we're going to make some gelt (Yiddish for money) here in Miami." Malcolm was excited.

"Which ever of you three marketing guys hits your six month goal; I'm taking for a week end to Las Vegas." I announced.

"Mr. V. I have no problem with that, but let's not go to the MGM casino."

"Why is that?" I asked.

"Because the last time I was there I found out what MGM means... My Gelt is Missing," he laughed.

Malcolm was the only rep to meet his six month goal thanks in large part to Manuela' s agency. So we went to Las Vegas as promised ... unfortunately we found that it wasn't just at the MGM where our gelt went missing.

CHAPTER 23

———•———

"WHO IS THIS ASSHOLE?" A medium build six foot four man said as he charged into the partner's office of one the largest Miami agencies.

I was being set up but I didn't know it at the time. Malcolm and I were meeting with one of the agency partners when the six foot plus individual charged into his office. I stood up and answered without a second thought.

"This asshole is Paul R. VeHom, and to what asshole am I speaking?"

There was a loud silence... then outrageous laughter.

"I' m Stan Stein, the owner of this mad house...I like this asshole at least he has balls let's take him to the club for lunch."

Stan and I had an immediate bonding... a sense of simpatico. His 'club' happened to be one of the most famous international clubs in Miami... complete with hotel, condos, pools, tennis courts and a world class golf course, all located on Biscayne Bay. Even the luncheon fare was, like everything else, decadent. Broadway show tunes were being played in the background by a live pianist.

"You just open your business casualty files, send me out with your associate, I will place the case, and your agency gets all the commissions." I said.

As the waiter refilled my Vichy water, Stan looked at his associate and then at Malcolm.

"How the hell do you get paid?" Stan asked.

"I'm paid strictly from the over rides and business volume bonuses." I answered.

"From now on you stay here at my club in one of the penthouse suites when you come to Miami, and hold all your seminars here... that'll make your bonuses sweet." Stan smiled.

Did it ever; Miami is the place where image is everything. When I'd have lunch with agency owners or brokers at the club they were amazed. I would even close cases for them at the club. This was a real break.

I returned to Miami a week later and checked into my penthouse suite. Even though Stan had made the club available to me the company was paying for my expense account.

Wait till they see this one I thought.

"Hey VeHom, welcome back...we're going to a snazzy night club on Friday night so stay over...you're going to love it." Stan laughed.

"Let's do it." I said.

"Just like that...no problem?" Stan asked.

"Done and done Stan." I answered.

"I like that VeHorn, no bullshit, just do it...I can handle a yes or a no but not a maybe, or some damn weak ass excuse." Stan scoffed.

Stan and I were on the same page in nearly everything. He was a member of the bar in Florida, New York, New Jersey, and Nevada...that speaks for itself. At one time he was elected to be a judge. He said that made him too high profile, and besides he lost money being a judge. He was one of those people in life who was truly bigger than life... and life was never, never dull around Stan.

"What's your Zodiac sign VeHom?" Stan asked abruptly.

"Aires with a Scorpio rising sign and a Scorpio moon," I quickly answered.

"That was fast...sounds like you're really into it...so am I...really into it...so you have an Aires sun and a Scorpio moon... son of a bitch... I have a Scorpio sun and a Aires moon...that means we' re really compatible." Stan mused.

Stan went on to let me know that he had a client who is a famous psychic astrologer. He did n't take it seriously until she did some psychic readings and astrological work for him. He had her astrologically profile jurors especially in major cases.

"She was right way more than the law of averages...at first I wouldn't accept it...and then I found out about an attorney in New York City who uses her...I called him and he said 'pay her fee' it's the best investment you'll ever make." Stan was intensely serious.

He went on to explain how he would check out the charts through her of people he was going to do business with.

"She saved my gelt more than once…big time gelt…that reminds me, this week you're going out with my associate Michael, to place a big case…it's a specialty medical firm with forty six physicians… but I'll warn you the doctor who owns it is a little bastard…so good luck…we'll see how good you really are VeHorn," Stan smirked.

I got into Michael's white Cadillac Seville remembering that image is everything in Miami. He was a kind of quiet guy who was impeccably dressed. He carried a South American hand crafted alligator brief case to round out his GQ appearance.

"I'll introduce you, but you make the presentation." Michael said nervously.

I agreed and soon we entered the luxury medical building that housed Dr. B's offices. We will call him Dr. B since Stan had described him perfectly. Michael introduced me.

"This isn't my idea, Stan said I had to see you…a fucking insurance salesman." Dr. B sneered.

Stan was super right only he missed the rest of the description. Dr. B was little (maybe five foot three with lifts) and indeed a little bastard…an obnoxious arrogant little bastard. I respect people regardless their height (my grandmother was four foot ten) weight or circumstance. However if you choose to be an idiot then an idiot you are.

"So you're proposing ten million dollars in insurance on me plus a million on each of my doctors plus disability insurance on everybody...you god damn mother fucking pile of shit I ought to kick your hemorrhoid afflicted ass." (Those were his actual words).

I was taken aback, but I rather admired his colorful word choice complete with medical terms. Just then a miracle happened. In bounded a very well endowed fortyish lady who looked like she just left a fashion show. Her makeup was perfect and so was her hair.

"I was outside...I heard you...I heard you yelling you sawed off little piece of unmitigated shit." She screamed.

She then turned to me. This ' lady' was Dr. B's wife...now I knew what made him so mean. It was pretty evident as to who ruled the roost. She lowered her voice.

"How much life insurance did you recommend for him," she asked me.

"Ten million on him because that' s a conservative estimate of the business value," I said quietly.

"I already have a million with you as beneficiary dear," Dr. B said meekly.

"You miserable little cheap bastard, I'll teach you," she screamed.

Michael whispered, "Maybe we ought to leave."

I gave Michael a look of, ' ssshhhh, say nothing.'

"You write twenty million on this insufferable little piece of shit and make me the beneficiary... plus I want notification of every premium payment, which will be paid annually…what else did you tell him to buy?" Mrs. B. asked.

"He'll buy everything you said to buy, if Stan says he needs it then we' ll buy it. . .I own half of this practice." She said sternly.

"And if I divorce your worthless lying, cheating, slut chasing uncircumcised little mini dicked ass (exactly her words) I'll own it all," she threatened.

It turned out that his was my lucky day…for Dr. B…not so much. I later discovered that he had been caught after a private investigator took videos of his…well you know…what she said…and in color of course. Somehow I felt Dr. B. richly deserved every derisive name that was laid on him. Feeling sorry for him was not an option.

"Well that turned out rather well." I said to Michael

"Talk about perfect timing, I heard that she found out yesterday VeHorn."

Stan couldn't stop laughing. He said she wouldn't divorce him because she had too much to lose.

"He's been fooling around for years, and she was aware of it…only now she's hit forty and thinks Dr. B. will dump her…from this point forward she has the evidence and has him by the balls…his life's going to be hell." Stan chuckled.

This was only Wednesday and we were all going to the "snazzy" night club on Friday. Stan said there was a great dance ensemble at the club on Wednesday night and I should go.

As I entered the club lounge...muted blue lights reflected off the large swirl patterned wall mirrors. A thick mahogany horseshoe shaped bar warmly greeted the guests.

"What will it be sir?" The bartender smiled.

"A Bond martini," I replied scooting on to a bar stool.

"Shaken, not stirred, very good sir," the bar tender said placing down an elegant napkin.

Actually Bond really said shaken and not stirred in the book "On Her Majesty's Secret Service." He returned shortly, martini in hand, and placed it on the napkin. I said nothing about the book. Two large olives on a wooden pick were in the martini.

"My name is Tim; I don't believe I have seen you here before sir."

"Hi Tim, Paul VeHorn and this is my first time here...but I will be here on a regular basis, as a guest of Sam Stein."

"Very good sir, everyone knows Mr. Stein... is this regular choice of libation, Mr. VeHorn?"

"Mr. V. is good and no, my usual is a single malt and soda...I just felt like having a martini tonight."

"I remember the drinks of all the regulars, so when you walk into the lounge put up your index finger and I will know single malt scotch and soda...otherwise just sit down and order."

Tim was a real pro, and of course that type of service requires the appropriate gratuity. The dance ensemble was playing mood music as some couples danced. Others were sitting at tables alone or in groups. I noticed a very well endowed fortyish looking blonde in a little black dress heading straight for me.

"Hi, you remember me...Mr. VeHorn isn't it?"

It was just too good to be true. I could see a flickering flame of revenge in her eyes as she sat down. I had the feeling that I was going to be the one she had planned to satisfy that revenge.

"I certainly do...you were the charming lady I met this afternoon," I said with a big smile.

"I don't know how charming I was, but yes, my name is Ellen." She laughed.

'Canadian Sunset' was being played by the trio. Ellen and I went from small talk to couples talk. Her husband was a sore subject... but for me he was the gift that kept on giving.

"We were married about nine years ago...from his part of the world the trophy wife is a blonde haired blue eyed hottie...and I was it... what a farce...he could never take me back to his country...or meet his family...I knew that from the start and I could live with that." Ellen said as she stared into the past.

"Do you have any kids?"

"I have a boy and a girl from my very young first marriage...He was successful about ten years older than me...I was divorced for a couple years and let my ex have the kids except in the Summer... then I met Wal...that' s his nickname...he was the same age as my husband...Wal didn't want me, he wanted the image...like everyone else he was okay at first...not great but okay...he loved showing me off...it was all about him...his ego...he' d buy me expensive jewelry, clothes, and cars but that was only to make him look good," Ellen said sipping her drink.

"Didn't that make you angry?" I asked.

"Angry...it made me livid...I started to hate the little bastard...we had fights... finally he said that he could marry more than one wife in his country...I told him to try it and I would sue his ass off... he fears that more than anything...he sends too much money back to his country for his family there...but that's just to look like a big deal." Ellen's drinks were showing.

I tried to change the subject since Ellen was raising her voice, but Ellen wasn't finished venting.

"He got cheap with me, and I wasn' t having it... he spent over forty thousand dollars for his family members over there to go on a sea cruise...I was so mad that I flew first class to Innsbruck Switzerland on a shopping trip just to match the money he spent on that cruise...which I did with his credit cards." Ellen smirked.

"Is there any chance of him coming here?" I asked.

"Never...he doesn't like to be around ' those people' as he puts it... Of course nobody likes him...even the doctors in his own clinic... they don't stay very long...just the ones out of school and then they're gone."

At that point, Ellen took me by the arm and slipped around on her bar stool. Her dress slid up to slightly above her knees...as she put her left heel on the floor her legs opened. The room was dimly lit but just bright enough for me to see her inner left thigh.

Where her thigh top hose stopped there were no panties beyond that. I could see that her quim was smooth. She gave me a knowing smile as we both stood up.

"You're a very good dancer." She said pressing her braless breasts against my chest.

Only a few couples were on the club dance floor. Ellen dropped her hand from my waist and ran it down to my already erect cock and slightly squeezed. I could feel the pressure of her smooth shaven mons rub up against my shaft.

A full moon reflected off Biscayne Bay as we stepped down onto the veranda outside the club. The water was shimmering as a cool breeze floated up from the incoming tide. No one was in sight. Islands of palm trees were lightly swaying from their hiding places on the beach. Ellen removed her heels as we walked through the sand arm in arm. Shadows covered us as we stood with the palm trees between us and the now distant veranda. The ground was hard around the palms. Ellen placed her back against a palm and put her heels back on.

"I'm so wet for you I can't stand it," her now husky voice trembling.

Her moon glowing eyes were eight inches from mine. She lifted her dress and then placed her left leg around the back of my right thigh. I slowly ran my tongue around the inside of her lips then into her mouth. Ellen grabbed my left hand with her right and pressed it into her right thigh. I could feel her wetness all the way down her inner thigh. When I raised my hand to her mons and lightly touched her clit she shuddered. I suddenly dropped to my knees and ran my tongue into her quivering quim. Her legs were shaking as she moaned.

"Oh my god... oh my god," she whispered.

Suddenly she lurched and let out a louder moan. I could feel her cum cream flowing into my mouth. After I swallowed it I had a sweet after taste on my tongue. I then got up and turned her around.

"Bend over and grab the tree." I ordered.

"Oh my god... Oh my god," she kept saying.

I rammed my rod into her vag... she squealed...I then pulled it out and rammed it back in; over and over.

"Fuck you Wal...fuck you Wal... fuck you WaL"

I thought at first she was saying Paul, but she was saying Wal. Every time I rammed in my cock she said 'fuck you Wal.' That was her husband's nick name I had heard of a grudge fuck or revenge fuck before but this was my first.

"Aaaaagh," Ellen made one long yell.

The inside of her vag suddenly gripped around my rod. I could hear a loud low moan like someone in pain. I didn't realize it was me. All I could think of was ' it hurt so good.' It didn't really hurt but it was like a firm handshake. That was how she had orgasms every time we had sex after that. We were exhausted... I sat with my back against a tree with her head on my chest and her arm over my right shoulder. Her open nipples were still erect as I fondled them while we talked.

"I think I am the victim here...I really feel victimized." I said with a straight face.

"What do you mean?" She seemed worried.

"You definitely used me to get even... that was a revenge fuck." I said laughing.

"You are bad...You're not nice." Ellen laughed.

"I told you, I'm not nice but I'm fun."

Ellen and I had only a few more encounters after that. Spring gave way to Miami heat and she went to Hyannis Port where her family had a place. She spent every summer there with her kids.

We didn't see each other again, but by then the affair had run its course. As the poet Robert Herrick said: ' Gather ye rosebuds while ye may.' Life goes on.

CHAPTER 22

———————

"HAPPY BIRTHDAY TO YOU, HAPPY birthday to you."

Fifty plus people were singing to Stan in the auditorium of his offices. He knew how to throw a party and we threw one for him.

"What's this VeHom?" Stan asked.

"Well, it's your birthday so I brought you a present." I said

Stan opened the wrapping on a twelve pack of his favorite European beer. You never knew what to expect from him.

"Son of a bitch...thanks VeHorn!"

With that he marched up to a small stage in the auditorium with the twelve pack and turned on the microphone.

"You cheap fucks... you come here... you drink my booze... you eat my food.. .it's my birthday and nobody brings me a present...except VeHom... the only one who doesn' t have to suck up to me...the rest of you should be sucking up especially some of you attorneys on staff." Stan was on a roll.

He said it in a half kidding half serious way, but he made his point. After the party which was held in the evening until about eight Stan and I went to the club. I was staying there for a week in one of the four penthouses as usual. Naturally my company was gladly picking up the tab since I now had the number one region in the nation. I took Stan to dinner for his birthday.

"You know what I mean VeHorn...I was serious about what I said at the party... a lot of attorneys are nothing more than educated derelicts... and most of them drink too much... when I was elected judge here in Miami I found out why lady justice had a blindfold... so she did n' t have to look at those idiots...they' re not all bad but the majority of them are just glorified law clerks... when it comes to wills, trusts, powers of attorney, health care surrogates, pre nuptial agreements and more they just take them down from an internet service, fill in the blanks, and charge huge mark ups." Stan said philosophically.

"You didn't go for re-election?" I asked.

"I couldn't wait until it was over; besides it cost me money."

For all of his bravado Stan had a certain sense of right and wrong that was really surprising. He did pro bono work that was purely a matter of how he felt about it.

"Have you ever been to a topless dance club?" Stan smirked

"Are you kidding...I live on the West Coast of Florida the home of the best."

"Well get ready because next Monday you're going to be dancing baby." Stan laughed.

"Excuse me?" I was dumbfounded.

"One of my clients has a topless club and Monday night is ladies night…amateur guys dance for the ladies…and if you don' t win you haven't got a pair…I've already sent out invitations…and all the ladies on my staff will be there…and I'll be there so you better be good."

"I always wanted to do something heroic in my life… this isn't it but it damn sure sounds like fun." I said shaking my head.

"I knew you'd have the balls to do it."

I flew down to Miami on Monday morning and arrived at Stan's office around ten. When I walked in I was met by the ' Rocky' theme blaring through the building, a long poster across the reception area which said "Shake Your Booty Baby!" and applause. Bets were being placed with the odds in Stan's favor.

"Hey VeHorn, you want to give it a practice run for us?" One of the stout ladies yelled while they all laughed.

"You'll see it tonight and you honeys better bring some money… I don't want to see all ones I want to see some Lincolns and Jacksons and even some Benjamins." I yelled.

I went to Stan's office where he briefed me about the performance of the year. He told me to wear black bikini underwear for the show. I said that was my plan.

"So what's in it for me?" I asked.

"I set this gig up as a charity for the Children's Hospital…so you will have a lot of charity type ladies at the show…When you come out the announcer will say that should you win any place you're donating winnings to the cause."

"Okay, so what are the prizes?" I asked.

"First prize is fifteen hundred, second is one thousand and third is five hundred…and this is the best part…you get to keep all the money they stick in your bikini or throw on stage because they'll want to watch you bend over." Stan was laughing like hell.

"I think you're going to have way too much fun tonight Stan."

On the night of the big show I was ushered in through the stage door. The music was booming and the ladies were chanting, 'we want the dancers, we want the dancers.' I never heard guys at a topless club chant like that. It was surreal. A lot of these ladies were society types promoting the children's hospital. I think women are a lot kinkier than men ever thought about being; they are just quieter about it…until they get into a group…at that point a sort of ' feeding frenzy' takes over…a mob psychology.

"Are you nervous VeHorn?" Sam, the club owner asked.

"Actually I am kind of surprised; I didn't expect the ladies to be so wild Sam."

"Believe me they can be worse than the guys… the more they drink the wilder they get… but not to worry, I have bouncers in case they get too far out of line… by the way don' t be surprised if they grab your shvontz when they put money in your bikini."

All six amateur performers were decked out in sexy outfits except for me. They didn't look like amateurs but that was what they claimed. One guy looked like a body builder; another was a dentist, while the other three were of various occupations. Then there was me. My garb was right off the street... grey suit, white shirt, black tie, laced shoes, black sunglasses, and a black hat pulled down over my eyes...and the black European style bikini which was all but see through. I also requested a straight chair be placed on stage.

"So why do you want a chair VeHorn...only the girls use chairs...oh yeah, okay I get it."

Sam chortled.

"Hey Sam what number am I going to be." I yelled at Sam back-stage over the music.

"Yer gonna be the last stud to dance...Stan's orders." Sam laughed.

So Stan had this all planned; he was going to wait until the ladies were in heat and then put me on last. I got to select my music, so I picked the Rolling Stone's ' Satisfaction.'

Sam introduced me over the microphone and suddenly the music started to roar..."I can't get no satisfaction." There I was in front of God and everybody...it took a few seconds for it to register that the roar wasn't just the music...it was a combination of the music and a theater full of turned on, tuned in, boozed up women...Oh my god it felt like my first day at boot camp.

I watched the other guys dance from the side off stage. They were all fast, jerking their clothes off while they were bumping and grinding. I decided that I would do something different. Sam had a standard black umbrella so I borrowed it for my act. I walked a determined walk across the stage to the center... all the while using my umbrella as a walking cane... I then stood in the center with the umbrella point on the floor and both hands on the handle. I just stood there for a moment looking at the crowd. The audience became silent. I then stuck the point of the umbrella straight up with my right hand toward the ceiling... the audience roared... then I took both hands and put it behind my back... as I started to move... slowly, deliberately side to side. All my movements were sensual and precise, not loud or fast. I then put my umbrella on the back of the chair and wedged it so the point stuck straight up... the ladies began to scream.

"Take it off baby, take it all off!" Women were yelling.

I removed my coat slowly and then flung it across the stage...then the tie... unbuttoned the shirt slowly all the while slowly gyrating my hips...then I ripped the shirt off and threw it on the stage floor...I put one foot on the chair which was facing the audience, gyrating all the while as I unzipped my pants...I then quickly sat on the chair and jerked off my slacks right over my shoes. Finally, my hat, my sunglasses my black bikini briefs, knee length socks and shoes were all that I had on.

"Anybody want to see me dance," I yelled as I danced toward the center of the stage.

I heard ladies screaming as I twisted, turned, and humped. The whole time I had my hands behind the back of my neck, then on my hips, then ran them up and down my body. The stage lights were too bright to see far beyond the stage, but suddenly up close there was a surge of bodies holding folding money.

"Go down the runway VeHorn," I heard Sam bellow over the screaming women.

As I tried to move down the runway... women were grabbing my legs...pushing money into my bikini...and feeling my cock and my ass while they did. Talk about getting a handful, my cock felt like a slot machine handle. I think some of them were trying to make change in my bikini. Later I even found money and telephone numbers tightly wrapped in panties stuck in my bikini and on the runway. I wound up picking up mostly fives, a lot of ones, tens and twenties. I kissed them if I saw a five or above or if they handed me money wrapped in panties.

"Here man," Sam said as he ran out on the runway with a bag.

Sam already had stuffed money and panties into the bag. Stan was right; the last dancer got the most tips, because the ladies were ready. Stan took a lot of pictures and had one of the ladies take a video. Unfortunately one of my ex wives, a jealous sort, threw the pictures away. I never did get a video although I did watch it when Stan had a "showing." Who knows...maybe one day they will show up on the internet. Let me know if you see it. I kept my hat, sunglasses, knee length socks and shoes on the whole time. That might give you a clue.

"Hey my man you came in second place...and picked up a lot a loot." Stan was ecstatic.

As we drove back to the club from Sam's theatre, Stan was in his glory. The other guys in the car wanted to know how many phone numbers I got. Over all they were they were having a ball.

"I' ll let you know how many phone numbers I have after I get rubber gloves to unroll the panties." I laughed.

The Children's Hospital charity had quite a successful evening making in excess of ten thousand dollars. My evening was also successful with a second place win and a thousand dollar donation to the Children's Hospital. I wound up with eleven phone numbers and over eight hundred dollars in tips. I didn't call the phone numbers, but I did donate the tips to the charity. As a footnote, Sam found out later that the first place winner was in fact a pro who danced in clubs throughout the country...oh well... life goes on.

CHAPTER 24

———◆———

ON OUR WAY TO VEGAS, the pilot tipped the plane to both sides in order to let the passengers see the Grand Canyon. Stan took me and members of his staff to Las Vegas for a job well done. Our group included his agency associate, a loser attorney from the firm... Stan's whipping boy... a big name politician and me. So there we were.. .five people going everywhere as a group... kind of like Stan's 'guys.' I always love to visit Vegas... for me it's nothing less than Disney World for adults.

"Hey dummy, I bought you a book," Stan said to the loser lawyer.

At best this joke was a legal ' gofer' or law clerk, but I guess Stan got him at the right price. He must have been a mental masochist since he ate up all the crap that Stan dished out. I was later to find out that he really was a jerk. He had been disbarred for committing fraud. Stan put him on staff with the bar association and criminal court's permission to do all the legal work for pro bono cases. Stan arranged this as a community service sentence instead of jail time so he did this guy a favor. It was supposed to be for three years but could continue in order for the loser to pay restitution.

"Oh thanks Stan." The loser smiled as he opened the wrapper.

The name of the book was something like ' Legal Information for Idiots' or dumbasses or some such title. We all laughed when he saw the ' gift.'

"You're going to learn how to really play craps VeHorn," Stan said as we strolled into the gaming area.

The casinos had no windows in the gaming areas so you so you couldn't tell if it was day or night. Stan ordered ' markers' for ten thousand dollars each. I didn't even know what a marker was until he told me that they were like a secured loan based on your credit worthiness at the casino. We joined the ring of players around one of the crap tables. The crowd was in a loud mood. The action was hot...made more raucous by a frenzy of orders being yelled at the dealer.

"Hard eight...hard eight...fifty on the hard eight...put fifty on the hard eight VeHorn."

Stan was giving me orders as well. The shooter had just rolled a five and a three so Stan wanted us to bet a hard eight meaning two fours. It was all confusing at first, but when the hard eight hit I quickly got what it was all about.

"Winning isn't everything, it's the only thing," Stan yelled.

I recognized that phrase, since the famous Vince Lombardi coach of the Green Bay Packers used it. Stan had a lot of expressions that he lived by. 'Never let them be throwing dirt on your coffin with you saying I wish I had done this and I wish I had done that' was another one among many... but they all made sense.

"Let's walk outside; I want to get some white powdered sugar donuts for tonight."

I couldn't believe that he was going to get those... but I found out later what he had in mind. He had been ' comped' a huge suite of rooms for us at the casino. We each had our own bedroom with the common areas being a living room, a kitchenette and a small study. After we all settled in, I walked into the kitchenette where Stan was busy shaking the white powdered sugar from the donuts off on to a sheet of tin foil.

"Hey, what's that all about?" I asked.

" You'll see." Stan said as he laughed.

The casino had six restaurants. We selected the Italiano Restorante, an Italian restaurant for connoisseurs...magnifico...was the only word to describe it. Not only was the wine imported from Italy, but the statuary in the restaurant was as well. A famous male singer came in with his entourage and came over to say hello to Stan... who introduced all of us... every time I hear the song ' New York New York' I recall that moment. It was already about nine P.M.

"Table time... let's go." Stan said leading his group.

The casino was rockin' and rollin' the dice were sizzlin' and the crowd was having way too much fun. So much fun in fact that I had to play the slots for a while in order to find a spot at the crap table where Stan was playing... and winning. The slot machine I was playing was okay, but no great shakes. While I was playing, ' Stupid,' the loser lawyer came over.

"Hey you gotta come now; Stan wants you over at the bar." He said excitedly.

Ever have that inner voice tell you to do or not do something? Well, something told me to keep playing that slot for a little while. As we were walking away, we heard bells ringing at that very slot I was playing, while a man and a woman were screaming. I had walked away from a twenty five thousand dollar jackpot. The worst part was that Stan hadn' t gotten to the bar yet where we were to meet. I really detested that loser lawyer after that.

"Come here, I want you to meet someone... this lovely creature's name is Elm...like in the tree." Stan said proudly.

Now call girls or escorts serve a definite need in a society. I have always respected their vocation as long as they are not being used or abused or extorted by pimps. On a scale of worth I see escorts at a much higher level than many in society. Although there are those who are higher on the scale...I put call girls above such scum as Wall Street manipulators... who never see jail time... pimps who get away with it. ..and finally politicians who are praised for their phony patriotism ...I rate politicians at the same level as pimps because that's all they are; they do nothing more than pimp for multinational corporations and special interests...just for the almighty buck...screw the voters...screw the middle class...they can buy all the liar ads they want in order to get into office...and buy all the political pundit liars for hire they need...and finally of course are men or women of the cloth who abuse children...that is my descending order of placement on the social scale.

"Hi guys," Elm said in a warm low voice.

She really was attractive, with auburn hair and green eyes. Her dress matched her green eyes; that must have involved some selective shopping. The other guys all said ' hi' but I simply smiled. Stan had arranged for Elm to be our entertainment for tonight.

When we got to the room Stan told everyone to have a drink, then motioned for me and Elm to go into the kitchenette. After we closed the kitchenette door Stan opened the tin foil and placed it on the table, he carefully made lines in the powdered sugar with a credit card. He then tightly rolled up a hundred bill to use as a straw.

"Hey VeHorn, this is just for you, me, and Elm...I brought this from Miami... don't tell the other guys about it." Stan smirked.

I took the first line since I knew what it was. Although I have never had it I acted like people did in the movies after they have a snort. I coughed and rubbed my nose. I definitely felt that an Oscar was in order for this performance. I did two lines and then Stan did two lines. He did an even better act than I did because he had been there on occasion. Then it was Elm's turn; there were three lines left.

"I'm high already; I've been there twice this afternoon with some really strong nose candy."

"Well, this is from Miami...the best...except it has been cut a lot... but it's real smooth...try it you'll like it." Sam coaxed.

I realized when we met her that she was on cocaine high. Elm quickly snorted all three lines then rubbed her nose.

"Oh baby that is smooth...whew that's good good good... let's have some fun time now." Thankfully Elm was already high.

The placebo effect is real. If I ever had any doubt, Elm proved the validity of that theory. Before we left the kitchenette, Stan made his monetary arrangements. The politician would be first with the full treatment, his associate would be next with the full treatment, Stupid would be third with a hand job and she would spend the rest of the night with me.

Stan was in a committed relationship and didn't participate. He really had integrity. I was divorced so I had no problem.

"Here's the deal...you do each one in their bedroom...one thousand each...for the lawyer I'll point out later a hand job for three hundred...and do him quick...he's an idiot...then fifteen hundred for VeHom here....spend the night with him...and wear his smart ass out." Stan had spoken his orders.

The three of us walked out of the kitchenette back into the living room. As soon as Elm got into the living room she stripped... slowly...first the dress slipped down over her slender body... she was wearing a green open nipple bra which was really erotic...I hadn't seen one since I was in Europe...then she slowly removed her bra, all the while smiling and cupping her orbs... she had on a matching green garter belt attached to dark hose.. at last she slipped off her sheer green bikini panties revealing her clean shaven quim... and there she stood in her four inch black heels garter belt and hose...We must have all gotten a hard on in unison.

"Okay here's the pecking order...or fucking order if you will...She takes (the politician) to his room first...then she comes back out after he's done...then (the associate) she comes back out after he's done...then you (he pointed to the jerk)...you get a hand job... wait a minute... you're right handed ... Elm give him something different...use your left hand on him."

We all started laughing at that one...except for the jerk.

"You mean that's all I get...why does VeHom get it all?" The jerk whined.

"You idiot, VeHorn brings more money into the firm than any two of my attorneys put together...you're lucky I don't make you do your own hand job." Stan smirked.

Elm took the politician into his room first. In the meantime, the rest of us talked except for the loser lawyer who was pouting and feeling sorry for himself.

"Those nipples on her got my attention, that's one reason why I picked her. I didn't even know they made open nipple bras." Stan mused.

"Oh yeah, that's hot...they pull the nipple out of the opening so they stand up and the circular opening is smaller so they stand out like thumbs.. .put a cotton or even better a silky top over them and voila," I said.

"Son of a bitch that sure got my attention...when she took off the dress her nipples even looked bigger." Stan was overwhelmed.

"French soldiers came back from what they called Indochina with Asian wives. A French doctor said that from puberty on a vacuum like device is placed over the nipple to make them stand out... he showed one to me which looked like a little cup with a valve on it.

He uses them for women who have inverted nipples, but a lot of women use them to enlarge their nipples."

"I'd sure like to get a set of those," the jerko said.

We all laughed and told him he'd really get noticed at the beach. Of course that's not what he meant but he just set himself up...

at least for derisive laughter...which men can be really good at. Naturally he had to live with that for the rest of the trip. Stan even bought him an "A" cup bra with the ends cut out and ' gifted' it to him at the casino bar.

"Okay guys, who's next?" Elm asked as she walked back into the room.

She really looked hot wearing the nylons, garter belt and heels. I asked her to put her bra back on and pull her nipples out.

"You like that VeHorn?" She cooed.

She did it perfectly... pulling her nips all the way out so the circle was snug around them. After a while they started to swell a little. She kept the bra on for a while and took the associate into his room. Nobody came back into the living room after she took care of them. She must have worn them out. It took less than ten minutes for her to finish off the politician, and just a few minutes more for Stan's associate. She took the loser for his left handed job. Stan timed it from the moment she went into the bedroom with him until she came out.

"Fantastic, you choked his chicken in six minutes...I love it." Stan gasped he was laughing so hard.

Well, I was set to be the next victim so to speak, and Stan was in his glory.

"Yer screwed now VeHorn...Elm I want you to fuck this smart asses brains out...got it?"

"Yes sir...come here Mr. VeHorn...I have a surprise for you baby." Elm teased.

She was probably in her mid twenties and looked perfect. But there was one thing I did not expect and no one noticed.

"I'll bet that you've never had a hot water gum job."

"I guess not," I said.

I was expecting that she was going to give me a blow job with hot water and gum in her mouth. But that wasn't quite it. She got up from the bed...went into the bathroom and came back to the bed, in the dim light I could see that she had something in her mouth... it turned out to be hot water...she then slipped her mouth over my rigid cock and started to suck...but she had no teeth only hot water and her gums...she had false teeth which she removed...the feeling was exhilarating...I was so shocked I just let go and squirted a load of man cream right into her hot water filled mouth...then she swallowed all of it and went back to the bathroom where she replaced her false teeth.

"That was a fantastic first for me...what happened to your dental work?" I asked.

"Well I don't do that for everyone... I had braces when I was a kid and the dentist fouled up... all my teeth went bad because of it and I lost them all when I was a teenager... my dad sued him for malpractice and won but I was left with only false teeth."

For Elm that first BJ was only for openers. She put me through every position she knew and some that I never even thought of. It was one big fuck fest. She was a thousand dollar a night escort...Stan gave her fifteen hundred for me...she said I made her earn it...Stan should have paid me...I think I earned it. She left the following morning after having had breakfast with us.

Elm said she would come down to Miami, but that never happened. We never saw her again...but I will never forget my hot water gum job...actually the only one I had ever gotten...before or since oh well...life goes on.

———◆———

CHAPTER 25

OUR COMPANY WAS TAKEN OVER by another, and our division was closed. The decision to sell out was so bad that the CEO and his team were fired within three months. I continued going to Miami on business as a broker, but not as often. One day I received a call from Stan.

"VeHorn, how soon can you come down," Stan sounded stressed.

"Any time you want Stan."

I got to Stan's office the next day and planned to stay for a week. When I walked into his private office, he got up to greet me, but rather slowly for him.

"Have a seat my friend, I have some rather bad news to share with you." Stan said in a low voice.

I sat down in front of his desk with a feeling of foreboding. My inside voice was telling me to prepare for what was to come. His eye contact with me at that moment was intense. He seldom called me Paul, but this time was different.

"Well, Paul VeHorn, we've had some great times...developed a friendship way beyond business.. .I want you to know that I place a high value on that...I don't choose to have many friends...I have a lot of acquaintances, but only a few friends...I love you like a brother." He said, his eyes welling with tears.

Stan put a tissue to his eyes, and paused before going on. He was right, we had outrageous times together. In many ways he was a mentor. He gathered himself together and then continued.

"I have about six months. The cancer started in the lung but then went to the brain. You recall that I was in the Navy. At that time the ships were insulated with asbestos which we now know causes mesothelioma resulting in lung cancer."

"Oh Stan, I deeply regret hearing that you have cancer."

"Yeah, well we already have a legal team in Admiralty Law...we're going to sue the bastards...unfortunately I won' t be around to see it through." Stan sounded like himself again.

"Let me take you to the Deli for breakfast." I said.

This was one of the most famous delicatessens in Miami. We had lox and eggs with bagels and cream cheese, sweet rolls in a basket and perfect coffee. We had a long talk over breakfast.

"In my life I've seen America change but not for the better...the infrastructure has had it and the politicians are a joke...there is no leadership, just a bunch of spineless bastards that suck up to the billionaires...during the Civil War, America under Lincoln built the trans continental railroad...I've been all over the world and the only place I've seen that doesn't have high speed trains is the U.S."

"You' re right...all over Europe, China, Japan, and even Thailand... Florida had a chance for rail and some damn Governor vetoed it... every time I drive from Florida's West Coast to Orlando or Miami the traffic is insane."

Stan said he wasn' t being cynical, just realistic. I felt that his bitterness was a matter of feeling helpless in both looking back and looking ahead to his fate. He went on.

" Teddy Roosevelt had America build the Panama Canal. Can you even fathom how these conservative idiots today would react to that...all they know is cut taxes for the super rich...for the love of god didn't' t anybody tell these assholes it takes money to make money...taxes are the price you pay for the privilege of living in America.. .If you don't like it leave. Can you believe that today's political imbeciles gave the Canal away?"

He was on a roll, and I was feeling his frustration. I told him he ought to write a book about how he has witnessed the decline of America. Stan told me to write it for him.

" VeHorn, it' s a disgrace that the most powerful country in the world is like a ship without a rudder...the god damned conservatives never had an original idea in their lives...what do you think the ' T' in tea bag party means?"

"Tea as in the kind you drink?" I said.

"Hell no, what do you think it means...the GOP and the tea baggers shut down the government twice...our country has never been shut down by a foreign power...but these brainless wonders did just that...and they reduced our triple ' A' credit rating.. .isn''t that treachery?"

Even though Stan came on a little strong, I couldn't disagree with him. Actually no one could. He made perfectly clear sense.

"I feel sorry for the people...they' re bombarded and brainwashed with advertising lies... too bad they believe it... it's sad...we need a third party or even a parliamentary system ... the founding fathers had no idea that this would happen...they couldn't even conceive of gerrymandering in order to keep a bum in office."

"The Franklin Roosevelt model was highly successful...I taught applied economics on the college level... Keynesian economics works." I said.

"Reagan was the worst president the middle class ever had...Old man Bush was okay in my book...he called Reagan's trickledown economics exactly what it was...voo doo economics...only thing that trickles down is piss and that was the beginning of the middle class being pissed on... I met with Milton Freidman when he was here in Miami...just a reed in the wind... his ' supply side' economics was now the official name for the tricklers...you can create a formula for whatever the powers that be want."

I could see that Stan was getting tired. I suggested that we go for a ride down to the passenger ship docks. He had been on over twenty cruises from the Caribbean to the Mediterranean. His favorite was an Alaskan cruise.

"Maybe I'll get one more cruise in before the end or the beginning if that's what it is." Stan said wistfully.

It was a balmy autumn afternoon. The breeze was picking up from the incoming tide. We left the boat docks and went to a beach park on the Atlantic Ocean side of Miami. We sat down on a bench under smoothly swaying palm trees. The waves lapped the shore giving a calming effect from the sea. It had almost a meditative effect as the fall sun cast long shadows over the sand. Stan was reflecting on his soul.

"I had my Bar Mitzvah in New York City at a famous reform synagogue there...like a lot of people, I drifted away from the faith...I don't really believe in religion...but I do believe in God...funny how at this time I start to think about that...I became a Mason and made thirty second degree in the Shrine...a lot to that."

"I didn' t know that...I'm a Mason.. .It's a type of religious experience for me." I replied.

"Not to be morbid, but I plan to have a Masonic ceremony, a military ceremony, a metaphysical ceremony, and a Rabbi to perform the final service...If your ass isn' t there I'll haunt you forever." He laughed.

"Sounds like a plan...I've been a Lutheran, a Catholic, a Zen Buddhist...and studied Judaism. The Masonic, military and metaphysical ceremonies are just right for me too. If I ever get married I' m sure my spouse will opt for a ceremony from whatever religion she may be. Who knows?" I said trying to lighten the mood.

We talked further. Stan was determined to have a sea cruise so he set up a four day cruise from Miami to the Bahamas. He said he was going to make it to the Virgin Islands but that neither of us would be allowed off the ship. A week after I returned home I got a call from Stan.

"VeHorn get down here Tuesday we're having a four day party." Stan laughed.

"A four day party, are you for real?" I asked.

"I' m throwing a party for all my friends on a four day cruise to the Bahamas...my going away party...I want everyone to remember it... you will be there." He ordered.

Of course I would be there. Stan was picking up the tab and taking only his best friends and their spouses or their significant others. I had neither, but he said I wouldn't be disappointed. Was he ever right.

The erotic scent of an Asian noir perfume wafted into the limo's back seat as the chauffeur opened the back door for her. She slipped her designer sunglasses down as she looked at me with a wry smile. A large white floppy brimmed hat with a beige scarf set off her thick gleaming black hair. High heel cork shoes perfectly matched her scarf. The off white low cut top swept up in the front just exposing her tummy. Her matching slacks were smoothly fit, but not too tight.

"Hello Paul, we've met before but I'm sure you don't remember... you were rather busy dancing at the time...in fact I put twenty dollars into your bikini." She said with that same wry smile.

"Oh my god you were there?"

"I' m so sorry... that wasn' t fair of me... allow me to start over... my name is AnnaBella." She smiled warmly.

"Of course you know that my name is Paul VeHorn...I' m somewhat at a disadvantage, but I hope you liked my dance routine."

"Mon ami, I loved it."

Stan selected this highly sophisticated wealthy widow who was for-tyish to be with me on the cruise. He obviously had superb taste. Annabella's accent seemed to be more European than Cuban. Her husband died less than a year earlier after a long illness. From all accounts she was totally committed to him throughout the ordeal. He was Belgium and owned a huge successful engi-neering corporation in that country. The entire fortune was now hers in trust.

"I am looking forward to being with you... the next four days will be so sexciting." Bella said as she reached over to hold my arm.

I wasn't sure if I heard her right or if that was her accent, but it did sound as if she said sexciting...I found out later...that's exactly what she said.

All four limos arrived at the cruise ship. Stan had made special arrangements for us to board without standing in the endless line. The chauffeurs were busy removing the suitcases. I noticed that Bella had one that was black aluminum with combination locks. I said nothing but it did make me curious.

" Mon ami this is fabulous", Bella said taking off her sunglasses.

This was not just a cabin, but a first class suite. Stan and his lady had one and he arranged one for us. This was a honeymoon suite with mirrors above the bed, a balcony overlooking the water and a variety of lighting colors including red and black lights. This suite even had two bathrooms.

"Report to the main deck life boat stations." The announcement was made with the life boat siren in the background.

After the obligatory lifeboat drill we returned to our suite. A magnum of iced Dom Perignon with two Champagne flutes was sitting on a tray filled with chilled shrimp, strawberries, and dark semi sweet Swiss chocolates. A single red rose was lying on the tray with a note. "Bella, only one rose since there's only one you... Paul." With that, Stan wanted to make certain that I had a fun filled four day cruise with the beautiful...albeit creatively kinky...Bella.

The Champagne cork hit the overhead with a vicious pop as the liquid foamed out of the bottle. We were both laughing as I filled the glasses.

"May your fantasies of today be your realities of tomorrow." I toasted.

"Mon Ami I like that, but let's have our fantasies today and tomorrow," she smiled.

As we started our second glass of Champagne and before we went to our respective showers... she opened the black aluminum suitcase and brought out a black silk robe and black slippers for me... then she carried her suitcase into the bathroom.

I finished my shower, slipped into the robe and slippers and sat on the king sized bed. The sliding glass to the balcony was open with the white sheer drapes slightly moving in the breeze. The sounds of a steel drum band on the back deck were drifting in. I got up to close the glass sliding door and room darkening drapes. When I turned around I saw Bella standing there with a black sheer knee length robe, wearing heels and nylons with a black and red garter belt. Her hands were behind her back.

"I want your lips...come here," she said in a whisper.

I went to her and smoothly, slowly, kissed her on the lips. My cock was already hard as she pressed her Mons against me... as I reached around her back I felt something hard covered with fur around her wrists... handcuffs...she had put them on herself. I felt a handle in her hand.

"Take the whip," she said in a breathy voice.

I didn't know what was coming next...although I almost did...as I took the whip she sat on the bed. The ' whip' had a long handle with about a six inch leather tongue as a paddle. Bella opened my robe with her lips and teeth and slid her mouth over my now throbbing cock. She placed her mouth only over the head and slightly behind it, rapidly moving her tongue beneath the sensitive spot under the head. She then slipped my cock out of her mouth and ran her tongue up and down the shaft...and then suddenly stood up, turned around, and kneeled on the bed with her face to one side lying on her right cheek.

"Mon Ami, paddle me... hard please."

Her lightly tanned bottom cheeks were exquisitely framed by her red and black garter belt. I could see her clean shaven now wet vaginal lips below. I smacked her with the paddle.

"Harder... harder," she moaned.

I smacked her harder...I thought... but not hard enough.

"Harder you son of a bitch...harder." She demanded now

I really got into it after that whacking both cheeks a half dozen times.

"Oh my god...oh my god...that's it...oh my god...fuck me.. fuck me."
Bella squealed .

With that I rammed my cock into her quivering quim...pulled it
out and rammed it in again over and over. All the while Bella is
squealing 'more, more' then suddenly she let out a loud long yell.

"Aaaaaaaaaaaaaah!"

I felt her inner walls grip around my cock... at that moment I had a
screaming orgasm...it was beyond belief...I felt like I was out of this
world...I could only hear her and myself way in the background...
when I came back into myself I heard her crying and sobbing...I
was still somewhat hard and kept pumping...I stopped when I
heard her crying.

"Bella, are you okay?"

"Oh baby I'm fine... that's just the way it is with me... it was
wonderful...I loved it." She said still whimpering.

Bella explained to me as we lay in bed completely exhausted, that
she has a complete emotional release when she climaxes. Her turn
on is bondage and discipline known as B&D...she always cries when
she has an orgasm...and sometimes she even cries before and during sex.

"Mon Ami, I am a devout masochist." She said.

"Well that certainly trumps being a devout Methodist," I quipped.

We dressed for dinner in dressy casual cruise ship style. Bella wore
an off white Grecian style dress set off by a gold colored metal and

leather belt. Her cork high heel shoes matched. I found out later that the belt and shoe set was a famous Italian designer's creation. Although the dress wasn't see through her open nipple bra left nothing to the imagination as to the structure of her nipples.

"You missed the first round of drinks VeHorn," the politician in the party said as we sat down.

Stan had reserved a separate dining room for our party for the entire cruise...very private and very exclusive. On one side the sea was in full view. The other three sides had mirrors and framed bas-relief sea scenes. Stan sat at the head of the table of course and he was already 'holding court' before we arrived. At the moment he was extolling the virtues of stupidity.

"The British couldn't do it, the Confederates couldn't do it, the Nazis couldn't do it, the Communists couldn't' t do it, but the god-damned conservative Republicans did it. As a veteran I am outraged that they shut down the government. Gingrich, that fat little bitch, was speaker of the house when they shut down the government. I've flushed better piles than him. He's the kind of kid in school who would get his ass kicked all the time. Hell, I used to be a republican but I changed parties when I was a judge. I had enough of Nixon. When I'd see him at Rebozo's place... he was mostly drunk and ranting about some damn thing. You know what conservative means? Conserve the wealth of the wealthy. All republican conservatives do now is to pimp for the billionaires."Stan was on a roll.

"Stan you can't believe all that, what about the voting public?" The politician asked.

"The masses are asses. Spend enough money on lies and they'll believe it. Joseph Goebbels the Nazi propaganda chief said 'tell the big lie and tell it often enough and the people will believe the lie'. People vote against their own interests. Some religions tell them contraception is a sin, or abortion, or gay marriage, or whatever, so they stupidly vote against it. The best thing is to vote against the candidate that has the most money. Get real; mega political dona-tions are nothing more than bribes, pure and simple." Stan was starting to slur his words.

Thankfully the waiters brought in the main course. The conversa-tion drifted into subjects other than religion or politics. Fashion was a big topic for the ladies, while the men were talking about real estate investments in Miami. Suddenly there was a pause as Bella mentioned some investments she had just made.

"I bought three pre-construction priced condos at three downtown high rises." She smiled.

What a coup. The timing was perfect and the result was that she more than doubled her money. Bella was immediately the cen-ter of attention. Everyone wanted to know how to get in on ' the ground floor.'

"I have options on three others...my stock broker told me it was a bad idea, but he's been wrong so often I felt that it was a good idea," Bella smiled.

The table conversation again drifted among various topics. Individuals were talking to each other. I could see that Bella was getting restless. She looked at me then her napkin ' accidentally ' dropped to the floor. As I bent down under the table to pick it up I could see that Bella's panties were missing as she spread her legs to show off her freshly shaved smooth quim.

"Thank you Mon Ami...you are such a gentleman." She winked wryly.

Shortly after that we left for a ' walk on the deck' as we informed our party. It was nearly ten P.M. Stan made certain that we would be on the cruise during a full moon. The shimmering waves spread under the silver moonlight like tiny glasses of sparkling Champagne. Bella's eyes met mine as she turned and faced me. Her left hand guided

Itself down across my now swelling shaft. Her lips trembled as her tongue slipped into my mouth.

"Oh...oh Paul...I need you now."

Her left heel was on the bottom rail of the deck railing. We were in a more private darker area. As I moved the left side of her dress up with my right hand I could feel her deftly unzipping my fly. I could feel her guiding the pulsating head of my cock into her warm wet mons lips.

"Oooo," Bella moaned as she pressed in the thick head.

The sexual excitement for each of us intensified as the thought of being caught became more real with every sound. We muffled our voices during the fury of our joint orgasms. Her nails bit into the skin on the back of my neck as my hands roughly squeezed her butt cheeks.

"Oh my god baby that was a wild ride," I said breathing heavily.

"But not the wildest...wait til we get to the cabin." She responded in a husky voice.

The ship gently rocked from the Tropical breeze as we rushed and kissed and tripped along the passageway to our cabin.

"I'm going into the bathroom to change...get some things you like out of this suitcase...I'll be back shortly." Bella said, her voice shaking.

The leatherette "cat o' nine tales" was the first thing I saw when I opened the black aluminum case. Other discipline hardware was sorted out in three layers within the case. I didn't even know what some were used for. The other question I asked myself was if this is for me or her.

"I' m back for you love."

Was she ever. She wore black fish net nylons and a black shiny leather garter belt that glistened in the light which she had covered with a red scarf. A matching French bra was squeezing her orbs so tightly that they had already begun to swell.

"The safe word is halt said three times." She said, her voice now trembling.

"Safe word," I asked.

"You are going to punish me...do what you want to with me, but if l say halt three times you stop."

I suddenly got it. This was her ultimate turn on. The high quality ties, gags, ropes, cuffs and more were all there for her "pleasure." Fortunately I had learned enough from Tech to do it right. My first selection was a blindfold which I secured firmly. I found a pair of padded handcuffs and bound her hands behind her back. The next was a padded collar to which I attached a leash.

"Oh god...Oh god...I can't wait," Bella breathed heavily in a loud whisper.

I wasn't quite sure what I had found next, but it had two pieces of PVC pipe which were threaded so as to be screwed together. At either end, were attached two padded cuffs.

After I screwed them together it made sense. The cuffs were designed to be attached to the ankles. Bella later told me that it was a leg spreader designed by her husband.

"What are you going to do to me," she asked, in a low shaking voice.

At one time I used a German accent to tell a joke. She said it kind of turned her on because her husband had a similar accent and he would give her orders while he disciplined her.

"Ach yah... mein fraulein...zo you vould like to vind out?...Mmm?... schzowing ist bettah than telling," I said in a stern voice as I attached the leg spreader.

I saw a cleat on the wall of the cabin designed to hold up an extra bunk if needed. I took off the leash which was six foot long and attached it through the cleat and then snapped it back on her collar.

"Undt UR nipplez look zo lonely," I said as I pinched her swollen nipples.

"Oww... you bastard... you bastard!"

I could tell that she was really getting into her turn on... her nipples were hard and rigid... her breathing was heavy and her inner thighs were wet and glowing.

" Ach...nein... fraulein... ich been ein zon ova bitch," I laughed cruelly as I went back to her black suitcase .

A pair of nipple clamps which looked like clothes pins with springs was next. She could see nothing behind the blindfold, but only feel what was happening. First, I slowly sucked each of her nipples. I then began teasing them with a feather.

"Nooo... no.. .I know what's next." She said in a low agitated voice.

The anticipation of pain...even pain for pleasure is far more intense than the pain itself. Or so she had told me some time ago. Bella spoke of being helpless and having sex, but it didn't occur to me that it turned her on. We once went to a movie called "Nine and a Half Weeks" (9 ½ Weeks). Bella got super turned on during the show. That night we had wild sex. I missed it, but that was a clue of things to come

"Oh god you son of a bitch...oh fuck," was all Bella could say.

As the nipple clips clamped together, I expected her to say halt three times... but surprisingly that wasn't it.

"Oh baby spank me... spank me," she pleaded.

She was crying as I pulled an eighteen inch hard leather paddle from her "collection." This was not just a paddle, it was unique. It had an embossed padded handle so that the spanker wouldn't feel the sting. How thoughtful of the designer to spare the smacker of such an annoying discomfort. The paddle had "give" so as not to raise welts...an engineering masterpiece to be sure.

"Harder baby... harder...harder."

That's what Bella was saying even though she was crying. It was erotic and I was turned on but she was at the ultimate stage of turn on. My feeling was as one of being outside of the action watching. Everything seemed as if it was in slow motion...kind of like the slow motion you feel when you're in an accident. By now her cheeks were hot to the touch and pink.

"Now my nipples...hurry."

That's got to hurt I thought. I removed the clamps. When I lightly spanked her nipples she let out a low groan.

"Now paddle my pussy...hard...hard," she was crying and begging at the same time.

I smacked her smooth quim with the paddle hard. On the second whack I was shocked. Bella let out a scream...at the same time she had a squirting orgasm. It was so huge her knees nearly buckled. At that point I bent her over from the back...ammed my rod into her quim and I came in a screaming body emptying orgasm.

Later that night in bed we slept and then talked.

"That was the only time I ever saw you actually squirt when you make it." I said in a question like statement.

"It hurt so good...I rarely squirt but when I do it's like the whole world stops. Everything was just perfect. What you want to ask is... "Why." Some people enjoy pain in sex but for different reasons or so my psychiatrist says. My reason is guilt…I have so much …too much but that isn't the whole story. My father was very strict and he would spank me on his lap. It started to feel good when I would rub against his legs as he spanked me. One time, the last time, he suddenly stopped spanking me. He looked at me and then got up and walked away."

"Do you think he realized what was happening? "

"I'll never know…soon after that he sent me to boarding school. I think I had a passion for older men after that…he died while I was away at school… I was his favorite… and he was mine."

"I've heard about this from other women. I also understand from a psychiatrist friend that if a daughter loses a father at a young age either through divorce or death she will seek out more mature men to be with and marry."

"I' m not surprised…that's exactly what happened to me. I was thirty years younger than my husband. He was so sophisticated, mature, and intelligent that I couldn't resist. In fact I didn't want to resist. I wanted him."

"How did he respond to your bondage and discipline needs," I asked.

"He was never judgmental with me ever. Not in any way. In fact he was open…he was there for me in every way. He took care of my sex wishes without questions."

"Were you concerned about how I would react?"

"No way, you're too cool to do the judgment game. Besides, anybody who will do a male stripper gig can't be all good," Bella laughed.

The cruise ship docked in Miami and we all went our separate ways. I saw Bella a few times after that, but the Florida summer was coming and Bella left for her vacation home in the Alps. Unfortunately, all good things come to an end. The people we meet in the Gulf of our lives are like islands in the stream.

CHAPTER 26

———◆———

"PAUL, I HAVE SOME SAD news for you." Stan's girlfriend and now wife was on the phone. "He told me that he had a lot more time." I said in disbelief.

"I know, but he finally had heart failure which was probably a blessing; apparently it was quick."

Stan's wake was attended by the good, the bad and the rest. He didn't really attend a temple as such, but he did have a Rabbi for his last show and what a show it was. A few well known celebs came in from Vegas and a number of people who he represented back in the day. The latter kept a low profile, but provided some incredible floral arrangements.

"If you have a eulogy or a word to say about Stan feel free to come on up," the emcee announced.

Yes, Stan the Man had an emcee for his funeral as well as a bouncer. That's right, a big burly bouncer named Vito that he knew from Vegas. I kid you not, that was his name. If you knew Stan you wouldn't be shocked. The bouncer gave the first eulogy, and he cried. Stan was probably laughing his ass of on the other side.

"So my final order from Stan is that if anybody cries I am supposed to kick their ass. It's nuthin personal so don be mad wit me," he said as he was blubbering.

It was the funniest memorial I ever attended. Stan married his girl-friend of nearly twenty years when he knew that time was getting short. She gave the last eulogy.

"As most of you know, Stan had a pacemaker with an ICD or in dwelling cardiac defibrillator for about fourteen years. Which he requested be turned off since he was terminally ill. He said I don' t want to be jumping around after I'm dead as that ICD keeps kick-ing in. Now if your heart is close to stopping that ICD will kick in and shock your heart back to functioning. Kind of like a kick start or re-boot. I can tell you first hand that it's like being kicked by a mule because I've had both. Stan and I were having sex one night and I was on top...we were both at just the magic moment when all of a sudden that baby kicked in and gave both of us the best orgasm we ever had in our lives."

The crowd went berserk. It was almost ten minutes before she could start again. "We asked the doctor how could it be that I got shocked too. He said, 'well moisture conducts electric current.' The reason for the shock is that he needed a stent. He would say I saved his life and if it weren't for sex he'd be dead. So after that his favorite mantra was: "Have sex live longer"

The beauty of all this is that you can't make these things up. The events that happen in real life can be hilarious.

At this point you're probably asking yourself what the hell does all this have to do with "Free Love and Nickel Beer?" I'm glad you asked.

About a year after Stan passed I had to go to Miami on business. However, I had relatives, my cousin Charles and his wife Daphne visiting from Europe. I took them along with me. I'd work during the day and they could do the tourist thing.

"The first night we'll stay in Fort Lauderdale. I'll get two queen size beds so we can stay in the same room," I announced.

It was Spring break time and ' where the boys are' happened to be in Fort Lauderdale. Fortunately I made reservations always a month in advance. Now I knew this place on Lauderdale Beach that ran a special on nickel beer. A small plastic cup but from five to Seven P.M. beer was a nickel. In Switzerland where they now lived and worked a nickel beer was unheard of.

"Charles I' ll make a bet with you. I'll bet you one hundred dollars that I can get free love and a nickel beer in Fort Lauderdale."

"Oh, that is not possible. Okay we have a bet. I will happily take your money," Charles said in a gaming way.

We changed clothes and went to the nickel beer bar. It was packed so I paid the waitress twenty bucks to get us a table. We ordered nickel beer and Guacamole dip with tortilla chips. Tequila shots were the drink of the day and the college crowd lapped them up. An obviously inebriated lady was dancing near our table. She was wearing a string bikini.

Daphne was underwhelmed and said she would have on more if she wore two band aids and a cork.

"Hey, what's your name dancing girl?" I yelled.

She heard me and came over to the table. Being more than a little out of balance she almost fell in Charles lap. Daphne had no sense of humor about that.

"My name is whatever you want it to be," she slurred.

"" How about Gloria since you look glorious," I even winced at that one.

"I like it, Gloria is glorious. I'm here with two other girls from school but I lost them around noon today," she said haltingly.

I thought, yeah they probably lost you. I ordered another drink for her which she promptly slammed down, and she was slammed. Then she started to cry. It was all I could do to keep from laughing.

"I have no place to stay tonight, I can't find my friends."

This was just too good to be true. So I tried seriously to do the right thing. As we all know, no act of kindness shall go unpunished. Only this time it was different. I introduced all of us and told her that if she wanted to stay with us it was okay but she would have to sleep on the couch.

"Oh that's great but maybe just a little nap," our ' Gloria' slurred.

I told Charles and Daphne that I would take Gloria to the room and they should come up soon so that we can go to dinner. I took Gloria to the elevator to go to the room.

"I've been here for three days and no sex yet, I want some fun," she whined.

When we got to the room she wanted to go to the bathroom. I thought she was going to get sick. Suddenly she called me and opened the door. There she stood, bathing suit on the floor and every slender inch of her looking good.

"Are you sure you want to play?" I asked.

"You don't like me."

I was afraid she would start crying again. I assured her that I liked her and just wanted to make sure she was okay with it, and I didn' t want to take advantage.

"I' m going to take advantage of you," she laughed.

With that she pulled down my shorts and began sucking my cock. I slid out of my beach shoes and top.

"Hey, no blow job that's all I get here I want some fun too," she said.

With that I grabbed a condom and quickly slipped it on. ' Gloria' boosted herself up on the bathroom sink cabinet and drew me into her. Just as we got started Charles and Daphne came in. The bathroom door was open and there they stood watching us.

"Don't stop, I don't care, don't stop, I'm not done," 'Gloria' demanded.

I almost laughed, but when I looked over Charles and Daphne were starting to go at it on the far bed. They must have had just enough to drink, and when they saw us that was the tipping point.

" ooooh, ooooh, ooooh, ooooh" Gloria was coming hard and she sounded as if she were singing.

After I made it she and I both lay down on the near bed. The bet was complete. We ordered out and had pizza brought in. At that point ' Gloria' was all but passed out. The three of us went out to sight see since it was a beautiful full moon night. When we got back ' Gloria' was gone with one of the hotel's blankets a pillow a wash cloth and towel and soap. I gladly paid for the missing items at check out. Full moon days and nights are always bizarre.

"Paul, wake up, here's your hundred dollars. You were right, you win. We'll tell everyone back home about my wild man cousin's free love and nickel beer."

That evening I took Charles and Daphne to dinner at the club with the hundred dollars and more.

And so it goes in The Life and Times of Doctor Paul.

The End

EPILOGUE

A POLITICAL PUNDIT RECENTLY ANNOUNCED that America was changing. What a shrewd observation. No, America isn't changing, it has
already changed. Trying to go backwards as some political and
religious groups propose is absurd. It won't happen, so get over it.
On my shows I frequently say... 'if you don't believe in abortion,
don' t have one'...if you don't believe in contraceptives don't use
them'...'if you don't believe in gay marriage don't marry a gay'...but
for the love of God don't tell other people what to do.

The political extremists who shut down the U.S. Government plays
right into the hands of those who are enemies of America, and
those who hate America...the ignorance of these political extremists surpasses only their stupidity. Divide and conquer is the mantra of those who would defeat everything America stands for. So
ask yourselves, who really funds these groups and what is their real
agenda?

Relating the experiences of a youth growing up in Middle America
during the post WW II years was not without its dark politics either.
Senator Joseph McCarthy allegedly was a drunken tyrant who was
another extremist. He found a communist under every bed and in
every closet. He ruined thousands of lives during his witch hunt.
The brilliant playwright Arthur Miller wrote "The Crucible" after

being called to testify before the "House Un American Activities Committee'.

America has had a history of extremists who have created more problems than solutions. The Volstead Act brought. prohibition, which was a disaster. The criminalization of marijuana is another, albeit latter day, Volstead Act. The politicians will finally figure out that another source of revenue is needed since they gutted taxes in favor of corporations. Even police, fire protection and education are poorly funded. The state of Florida is 47th. in the nation for education funding. That other source of funding is quite simple... legalize and tax marijuana. As politicians look to Colorado's seven hundred million dollar marijuana tax wind fall they are asking themselves..." Why make drug dealers rich when we can improve our cities, counties and states with that revenue?" As always, it's all about the money.

Life goes on in America, but like the tide its fortunes ebb and flow.

A C K N O W L E D G E M E N T

—▪—

This acknowledgement is in memory of "Stan" who would happily haunt me if I didn't include his exact words regarding the Nixon curse. So to the best of my recollection the following is the complete context which "Stan" so emphatically (he'd love that description) delivered at his own 'Last Supper' on the cruise.

"Hell, I used to be a republican, but I changed parties when I was a judge. I had enough of Nixon. When I'd see him at Rebozo's place he was mostly drunk and ranting about some damn thing. Only one night his ranting was deadly serious. Nixon's war on drugs plan was formed that night right here in Miami. All of a sudden Tricky Dickey yelled..."Oh yeah I hate them (his word) goddamn hippies put pot on there too.' So the Nixon curse began. Marijuana became a class one narcotic for no reason whatsoever. Marijuana isn't an opiate, or even addictive like tobacco or alcohol. Millions of American kids and adults were jailed and lives were ruined for over fifty years all because of that miserable little troll. So that did it. After that how could I justify my judgeship? The cost was astounding both in lives and in taxes. So I resigned as a judge because I could no longer be part of that whole damn vicious farce.'

In a final salute to "Stan" I will share his favorite toast with you and one that I use in closing all of my shows…"MAY YOUR FANTASIES OF TODAY BE YOUR REALITIES OF TOMORROW!'

ABOUT THE AUTHOR

———◆———

DR. PAUL R. VEHORN, PHD, has held a variety of positions and tried on many different hats over the course of his career. He has served in the US Army, US Navy, joined MENSA, taught high school and college, worked as a stock broker, insurance broker and real estate agent, and entered the Screen Actors Guild!

VeHorn is also the nationally recognized host of *The Dr. Paul Show,* a talk show that focuses on troubled relationships. He has also appeared in two feature films and numerous television and radio commercials.

VeHorn is the author of *Dynamic Dating, Boomer Girls: A Woman's Guide to Men and Dating,* and *Free Love and Nickel Beer.* He holds a bachelor's degree in communications, business, and education. Having taken master's courses in education, he went on to receive his doctorate in behavioral psychology.

Facebook: doc@askdoctorpaul.com